FICTION HOUSE PRESS
PRESENTS

SUSPENSE Magazine

Summer 1951
Vol. 1, No. 2

This reprint edition is a facsimile of the original pulp magazine. Variations in printing and quality can be attributed to the original magazine which was printed on rough woodpulp paper. No attempt has been made to politically correct any language deemed inappropriate to the modern reader.

ISBN 978-1-64720-399-3

www.FictionHousePress.com
fictionhousepress@gmail.com

VOL. 1, NO. 2 SUMMER, 1951

THE HIGH-TENSION MAGAZINE

INSPIRED BY THE CBS RADIO AND TELEVISION PROGRAM SERIES *SUSPENSE*

SCIENCE FICTION

MYSTERY

ADVENTURE

CRIME

THE MACABRE

FANTASY

NOVELETTE

SUSPENSE Magazine is published quarterly by the Farrell Publishing Corporation at 350 East 22nd St. Chicago, Ill. Editorial and general offices at 420 Lexington Ave., New York 17, N. Y. Tom Farrell, president. A. E. Abramson, vice-president; Paul Thurlow, treasurer; Edwin J. Harragan, secretary. Entry as second class matter applied for at the post office at Chicago, Ill., under the act of March 3, 1879. Title registered in U. S. Patent Office and in Canadian Trade Marks office. Spring 1951, edition. This issue is published simultaneously in the Dominion of Canada. Subscriptions $1.00 a year, in the United States and its possessions and Canada. Not responsible for unsolicited material. Printed in U. S. A. Vol. 1, No. 2. Summer, 1951.

OPERATION

JOHN WYNDHAM

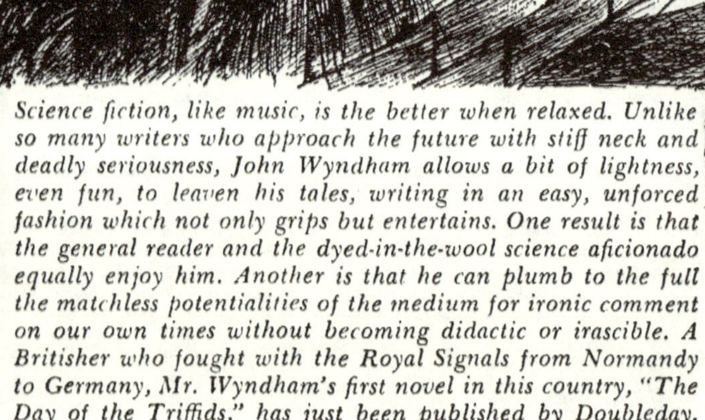

Science fiction, like music, is the better when relaxed. Unlike so many writers who approach the future with stiff neck and deadly seriousness, John Wyndham allows a bit of lightness, even fun, to leaven his tales, writing in an easy, unforced fashion which not only grips but entertains. One result is that the general reader and the dyed-in-the-wool science aficionado equally enjoy him. Another is that he can plumb to the full the matchless potentialities of the medium for ironic comment on our own times without becoming didactic or irascible. A Britisher who fought with the Royal Signals from Normandy to Germany, Mr. Wyndham's first novel in this country, "The Day of the Triffids," has just been published by Doubleday.

PEEP

SCIENCE SATIRE

With parts of people poking right through walls at most embarrassing moments, life became intolerable. Only an "invention" could restore precious peace and privacy . . .

When I called 'round in the evening I showed Sally the paragraph in the Center City News.

"What do you think of that?" I asked her.

She read it, standing, and with an impatient frown on her pretty face.

"I don't believe it," she said, finally.

Sally's principles of belief and disbelief are things I never could get a line on. How a girl can dismiss a pack of solid evidence like it was kettle steam. . . . Oh, well, skip it. The paragraph read:

MUSIC WITH A KICK

Patrons at Adams Hall last night got a shock when they saw a pair of legs dangling knee-deep from the roof while the concert was on. Seemingly everybody there saw them and all reports agree they were bare feminine gams. After three or four minutes and a couple of cute kicks they disappeared upwards. Examination of the roof showed everything normal, and the owners of the hall are at a loss to account for the phenomenon.

"It's just more of the same," I said.

"So what?" said Sally. "What does it prove, anyway?" she added, apparently forgetful that she wasn't believing it.

"I don't know—yet," I admitted.

"Well, there you are then," she said.

Sometimes I get the feeling Sally doesn't rely much on logic.

To me, it looked like there were things happening that needed adding together.

You see, Sally and I knew about the first guy to bump against it. A certain Patrolman Walsh. Oh, maybe others saw things before that and just put them down as a new kind of pink elephant. But when Patrolman Walsh found a head sitting up on the sidewalk, he stopped to look at it pretty hard. The thing that upset Walsh, according to the report he turned in after running half a mile to the precinct station, was that it turned to look back at him.

If it did, he shouldn't have mentioned it; it just naturally brought the pink elephants to mind. Nobody in a respectable police station wants to hear a thing like that. However, he stuck to his story, so after they'd bawled him out a bit and taken disappointing sniffs at his breath, they sent him back with another man to show just where he'd seen the thing. Of course no head could be found—nor signs of cleaning-up marks. And that's all there was said about the incident—save, doubtless, a few curt remarks on the conduct-sheet to dog his future career.

But two evenings later another queer story made the papers. Seems an apartment house was curdled by searing shrieks from a Mrs. Rourke in No. 35 and simultaneously from a Miss Farrell who lived above her. When the neighbors arrived, they found Mrs. Rourke hysterical about a pair of legs that had been dangling from her bedroom ceiling; and Miss Farrell the same about an arm and shoulder stretched out under her bed. But there was nothing to be seen on the ceiling, and nothing under the bed beyond a discreditable quantity of dust.

There were other little incidents, too. It was Jimmy Lindlen who drew my attention to them. He works, if that isn't too strong a word for it, in my office and his hobby is collecting queer facts. In this he is what you might call the *reductio ad* opposite *absurdum* of Sally. For him everything screwy that gets printed in a newspaper is a fact—poor fellow. I guess he once heard that the truth is never simple, from which he deduced that everything not simple must be true.

I've never actually seen Jimmy at work on his hobby. But at a guess I'd say he would deal himself a hand of cuttings in which there was one strange yet constant factor, discard the awkward ones, and then settle down to astonish himself as much as possible with theories about the rest. I got used to him coming into my room full of inspiration, and didn't take much account of it. I knew he'd shuffle and deal himself another hand that evening and stagger himself all over again. So when he brought in that first batch about Patrolman Walsh and the rest I didn't ignite much.

But some days later he was back with more. Maybe work was slack, or maybe I was surprised by his playing the same type of phenomena twice running. Anyway, I paid more attention than usual.

"You see. Arms, heads, legs, torsos all over the place. It's an epidemic," said Jimmy. "There's something behind it. *Something's happening!*" he said, as near as you can vocalize italics.

When I'd read the clippings, I had to admit that maybe he was right.

A bus driver had seen the upper half of a body upright in the road before him—but a bit late. When he did stop and climb out, sweating, to examine the mess, there was nothing there. A woman hanging out of a window watching the street saw another head below her, doing the same—but this one was projecting out of the solid brickwork. There was a pair of arms which came out of the floor in a butcher's shop, then withdrew into the solid cement. There was the man on an erection job who became aware of a strangely dressed figure standing close to him, but in the empty air—after which he had to be helped down and sent home. Another figure was noticed between the rails in the path of a heavy freight train, but had vanished without trace when the train had passed. The dozen or so witnesses agreed that it was wearing some kind of fancy dress, but looked quite masculine. . .

While I skimmed through the clippings Jimmy stood waiting, like a bottle of seltzer.

"You see," he fizzed enthusiastically. "Something *is* happening."

"Supposing it is," I conceded. "But what?"

"The manifestation zone is limited," Jimmy said impressively. "If you look where I've circled the incidents on this city plan, you'll see they're grouped. Somewhere in that circle is the 'focus of disturbance.' " He nicely managed to vocalize the inverted commas. "I've got a pretty good idea of the cause," he added, weightily.

I rarely knew Jimmy when he hadn't, though it might be a different one an hour later.

"I'll buy it," I offered.

"Teleportation! Busting a thing up and transmitting it through space like television sends pictures. That's what it is. Bound to come sooner or later!" He leaned forward earnestly. "How else'd you account for it?"

"If there could be teleportation, or teleportage, or whatever it is, I reckon there'd have to be a transmitter and some sort of reassembly station," I told him. "You couldn't expect a person to be kind of broadcast and then come together again any old place."

"But you don't *know* that," he pointed out. "Besides, that's part of what I was meaning by 'focus.' It may be focused on that area."

"If it is," I said, "it seems to have got its levels and positions all to hell. I wonder just what happens to a guy who gets himself reassembled half in and half out of a brick wall?"

It's details like that which get Jimmy impatient.

"Obviously," he said, "it's in the early stages. Experimental."

"Huh," I said.

THAT evening had been the first time I had mentioned the business to Sally, which on the whole was a mistake. After making it clear she didn't believe it, she went on to call it "just another invention."

"What do you mean. Why, it would be greater than the wheel!"

"Should be," she said, "but not the way we'd use it."

Sally was in one of her withering moods. She turned on that voice she reserves for the stupidities of the world.

"We've got two ways of using inventions," she said. "One is to kill more people more easily; the other is to help short-sighted goons make easy money out of suckers. Maybe there are a few exceptions, like X-rays, but look at the movies, listen to the radio, and can you or I go buy a nice cheap little helicopter to keep in the back yard?"

Sal gets like that sometimes.

"Inventions!" she said, with as near a snort as her snub nose can manage. "What we do with the product of genius is first ram it down to the lowest common denominator, then multiply it by the vulgarest possible fractions. What a world! When I think of what other centuries are going to say of us it just makes me go hot all over."

"You're a funny girl," I told her. "Future generations, hey? I suppose they'll laugh like hell at us—but at least we won't know it. And will they be doing any different with *their* inventions?"

A couple of days later Jimmy looked into my room again.

"He's laid off," he said. "This teleporting guy. Not a report later than Tuesday. Maybe he knows somebody's on to him."

"Meaning you?" I asked.

He frowned. "I got it figured out. I took the bearings on the map of all the incidents, and the fix came on New Saints Church. I've searched the place, but I didn't find anything. Still, I figure I'm close—why else would he stop?"

That very evening there was a paragraph about an arm some woman had watched travel along her kitchen wall.

When I showed it to Sally, later, she started to snort again. Quickly I suggested a movie. When we got out it was raining but Sally had on her slicker and we decided to walk back to her place. I took her arm.

"Honey," I said, "I know I am regarded as an irritating cluck with a low ethical standard. But have you ever seriously thought what an opportunity there is here for reform?"

"Yes," she said, decisively, and in quite the wrong tone.

"What I mean is," I told her patiently, "if you happened to be looking for a good work to devote your life to, what could be better than reformation? The scope is tremendous and—"

"Is this a proposal of some kind?" Sally inquired.

"*Some* kind! I'll have you know that in spite of my dubious ethics . . . good God!" I broke off.

We were in Tyler Street, rainswept, and empty now except for ourselves. What stopped me was the sudden appearance of a kind of vehicle farther along. I couldn't make it out clearly on account of the rain, but I got the impression of a low-built truck, with several figures in light clothes on it, crossing Tyler street quite swiftly, and vanishing. That wouldn't have been so bad if there were any street crossing Tyler, but there isn't: the truck just came out of one side, and went into the other.

"Did you see what I saw?" I said.

We rushed to the place where the thing had crossed, and looked at the brick wall on one side and the housefronts on the other.

"You must have been mistaken," said Sally.

"Well, for. . . *I* must have been mistaken!"

"But it couldn't have happened, could it?"

"Now listen, honey—you saw it, didn't you?"

But at that moment someone stepped from the solid brick, about ten feet ahead of us! A girl! We gaped at her.

I don't know whether the hair was her own, art and science can do so much together; but the way she wore it! Like a great golden chrysanthemum a foot-and-a-half across with a red rose in it a little left of center. She had on a kind of pink tunic. Maybe it was silk. It wasn't the kind of thing you expected to see in Tyler Street on a filthy wet night, but for sheer coverage it would have got by—well, maybe in a girlie show. What made it a real shocker were the things which had been achieved by embroidery. I never would have believed a girl could—oh, well, anyway, there she stood, and there we stood.

When I say "she stood," she certainly did, but somehow she did it about six inches above ground level. She looked at us both, then she stared at Sally just as hard as Sally was staring at her. It must have been some seconds before any of us moved. The girl opened her mouth as if amazed. She took out a piece of paper—looked like a picture of some kind—from somewhere. She gazed from it to Sally, seemed to laugh with delight, then excitedly turned, waving the paper, and walked back into the wall.

Sally stood quite still, the rain shining on her slicker. When she turned so that I could see her face under the hood there was an expression on it quite new to me. I put my arm around her, and found she was trembling. "I'm scared, Jerry," she said.

I was badly rattled myself, but she needed an act.

"No cause for that, honey. Bound to be a simple explanation—"

"But it's more than that, Jerry. Didn't you see her face? She looked exactly like me!"

"Not nearly so pretty," I argued nobly.

"Jerry, she was *exactly* my twin... I-I'm scared."

"Must have been some trick of the light. Anyway, she's gone."

All the same, it stood my hairs on end. That girl was the image of Sally, all right.

JIMMY came into my room next morning with a copy of the News. It carried a brief, facetious story on the number of local citizens who had been seeing things lately.

"They're beginning to take notice at last," he said.

"How's your research going?"

He shrugged. "I guess it's not quite the way I thought. As I see it, it's still in the experimental stage, all right, but the transmitter may not be around here after all. This may just be the area he has it trained on for testing."

"But why here?"

"How would I know?" He paused, looking portentous. "It *could* be mighty serious. Suppose some enemy had a transmitter, and could project things or people here . . . ?

"Why here?" I said again. "I'd think Oak Ridge, or maybe Brooklyn Navy Yard. . ."

"Experimental," he said, reprovingly.

I told him what Sally and I had seen the previous night. "She sort of didn't look the way I think of enemies," I added.

Jimmy shook his head. "Might be camouflage."

Next day, after half of its readers had written in to tell about the funny things they'd been seeing, the News dropped the facetious angle. In two days more the thing had become factional, dividing sharply into what you might call Modern and Classical camps. The former argued the claims of teleportage against three-dimensional projection or some theory of spontaneous molecular assembly: in the latter, opinions could be sorted into beliefs in a ghostly invasion, a suddenly acquired visibility of habitual wandering spirits, or the imminence of Judgment Day. In the heat of debate it was becoming difficult to know who had seen how much of what, and who was enthusiastically bent on improving his case at some expense of fact.

On Saturday Sally and I met for lunch. Afterwards we took the car *en route* for a little place up in the hills which seemed to me an ideal spot for a proposal. But at the corner of Jefferson and Main the man in front of me jumped on his brakes. So did I, and the guy behind me. The one behind him didn't quite. There was an interesting crunch of metal going on on the other side of the crossing, too. I stood up to see what it was all about, and then pulled Sally up beside me.

"Here we go again," I said. "Look!"

Slap in the middle of the intersection floated a—well, you could scarcely call it a vehicle—it was more like a flat trolley or platform, about a foot off the ground. And when I say off the ground, I mean just that. No wheels. It kind of hung there from nothing. Standing on it, dressed in colored things like long shirts or smocks, were half a dozen men looking at the scenery. Along the edge of the platform was lettered: PAWLEY'S PEEKHOLES.

One of the men was pointing out New Saints Church to another; the rest were paying more attention to the cars and the people. The cop on duty was hanging a goggling face out of his uniform. He bawled, he blew his whistle, then he bawled some more. The men on the platform took no notice. He got out of his box and came across the road like he was a volcano which had seen a nice place to erupt.

"Hey!" he bellowed.

It didn't worry them. When he got a yard or two away they noticed him, nudged one another, grinned. The cop's face went purplish; his language was a pretty demonstration of fission. But they just watched him with amused interest. He drew his stick, and went closer. He grabbed at a fellow in a yellow shirt—and his arm went right through him.

The cop stepped back. You could see his nostrils kind of spread, the way a horse's do. He got a hold on his stick and made a fine circular swipe at the lot of them. They just grinned at him as the stick went through them.

I'll hand it to that cop. He didn't run. He stared at them a moment, then he turned and walked deliberately back to his position; just as deliberately he signaled the north and south traffic across. The guy ahead of me was ready for it, he drove right at, and through, the platform. It began to move, but I'd have just nicked it myself had it been nickable. Sally, looking back, said it slid away on a curve and disappeared into the First National Bank.

When we got to the spot I'd had in mind the weather had turned bad; it looked dreary and unpropitious, so we drove around and then back to a nice quiet roadside restaurant just out of town. I was getting the conversation around to the mood where I wanted it when who should come over to our table but Jimmy.

"Fancy meeting you two," he said. "Did you hear what went off at Main and Jefferson this afternoon, Jerry?"

"We were there," I told him.

"You know, Jerry, this is something bigger than we thought—a whole lot bigger. That platform thing. These people are technically way ahead of us. Do you know who I think they are?"

"Martians?" I suggested.

He stared at me. "Gee! How did you guess that?" he said, amazedly.

"I sort of saw it had to come," I admitted. "But," I added, "I kind of feel Martians wouldn't be labeling anything 'Pawley's Peekholes.' "

Jimmy went away sadly.

But he'd wrecked the mood. My proposal waited.

ON MONDAY, our stenographer, Anna, arrived more scattered than commonly.

"The most terrible thing just happened to me. Oh my, did I blush all over!"

"*All* over?" inquired Jimmy, with interest.

"I'm serious! I was in my shower this morning, and when I looked up there was a man in a green shirt standing watching me. Naturally, I screamed at once."

"Naturally," agreed Jimmy. "And what happened then, or shouldn't I . . .?"

"He just stood there," Anna said, firmly. "Then he sniggered at me, and walked away *through the wall!* Was I mortified!"

Jimmy said: "Very mortifying thing, a snigger—and at you, too—"

"That's not what I—what I mean is, things like that oughtn't to be allowed," Anna said. "If a man's going to be able to walk through a girl's bathroom walls, where's he going to stop?"

Which seemed a pretty fair question.

The boss arrived just then. I followed him into his room. He wasn't looking happy.

"What the hell's going on in this damned town, Jerry?" he demanded.

"I'd like to know," I told him.

"Wife comes home yesterday. Finds two incredible girls in the sitting-room. Thinks it's me. First bust-up in twenty years. Girls vanish," he said, succinctly.

That evening when I went to see Sally I found her sitting on the steps of the house in the drizzle.

She gave me a bleak look.

"Two of them came into my room. A man and a girl. They wouldn't go. They laughed at me. Then they started—well—acting as if I weren't there. I-I couldn't stay, Jerry."

Then, not altogether accountably, she burst into tears.

FROM then on it stepped up. By the end of the next day the town was full of mothers crying shame and men looking staggered, and the mayor and the police were snowed under with protests and demands that somebody do something about it.

The trouble seemed thickest in that district which Jimmy had originally marked out. You *could* meet them elsewhere, but in this one area you were liable any and every minute to encounter a gang; the men in colored shirts, the girls with amazing hair-do's and more amazing decorations on their skirts, sauntering arm in arm out of walls, wandering indifferently through automobiles and people alike. They'd pause anywhere to point out things and people to one another and go into helpless roars of silent laughter. What tickled them most was when folks got riled with them. They'd make signs and faces at them until they got them tearing mad—and the madder the funnier.

You couldn't seem to be free of them any place in the area though they appeared to be operating on levels that weren't always the same as ours. In some places it looked as if they walked on the ground or the floor, but in others they were inches above it, and elsewhere you'd find them moving along as if they were wading through the solid surface. It was soon very clear that they could not hear us any more than we could them, so there was no getting at them that way.

After three days more of it Center City was in chaos. There just wasn't any privacy. At the most intimate moments they were liable to wander through visibly giggling and guffawing. All very well for the police to announce that there was no danger, that the visitants couldn't *do* anything, so the best way was simply to ignore them. There are times and places when giggling bunches of youths and maidens take more ignore-power than the average guy's got. It sent even a placid fellow like me wild at times, while the women's leagues of this-and-that, the purity promoters and the like were living in a constant state of blown tops.

The news getting around hadn't helped, either. News hounds of all breeds burned the roads into town. They overflowed the place. Pretty nearly every street was snaked with cables of movie cameras, television cameras and microphones, while the press-photographers were having the snappy-shot time of their lives.

But there was more to come. Jimmy and I happened on the first demonstration of it. We were on our way to lunch, Jimmy quite subdued. He'd given up theories on account of the facts had kind of submerged him. Just short of the lunch-bar, we stopped, noticing a commotion further along Main Street. After a bit, a vehicle emerged from a tangle of cars farther down and came towards us at some seven or eight miles an hour. Essentially it was a platform like the one Sally and I had seen at the crossing that Sunday, but this was de luxe. There were sides to it glistening with new paint, red, yellow and blue, enclosing seats set four abreast. Most of the passengers were young, though there was a sprinkling of middle-aged men and women dressed in a soberer version of the same fashions. Behind the first platform followed half a dozen others. We read the lettering on their sides and backs as they went past:

PAWLEY'S PEEKHOLES
INTO THE PAST

GREATEST INVENTION
OF THE AGE

HISTORY WITHOUT TEARS—
$10.00 A TRIP

SEE HOW GT. GT. GRANDMA
LIVED

YE QUAINTE OLDE
20th CENTURY EXPRESSE

EDUCATIONAL!
LEARN PRIMITIVE
FOLKWAYS & LIVING
CONDITIONS

VISIT ROMANTIC
20th CENTURY—
SAFETY GUARANTEED

KNOW YOUR HISTORY—
GET CULTURE—$10.00

BIG MONEY PRIZE—
IF YOU IDENTIFY
YOUR OWN GRANDAD/MA

That last one explained the mystery of Sally's twin of the ether.

I noticed that most of the occupants of the vehicles were turning their heads this way and that in gog-eyed wonder interspersed with spasms of giggles. Some of the young men waved their arms and addressed us with witticisms to the admiration of their companions. Others leaned back, bit into large yellow fruits, and munched. On the back of the next to last car was lettered:

HOW GOOD WAS
GT. GRANDMA?
FIND OUT FOR YOURSELF

SPOT THE FAMOUS—
SHARP EYES MAY WIN YOU
A BIG PRIZE

As the procession moved away it left the rest of us looking at one another kind of stunned. Nobody seemed to have much left to say just then.

I GUESS that show must have been something in the nature of a grand premiere. After that you were liable almost any place about town to come across a platform labeled HISTORY IS CULTURE—BROADEN YOUR MIND, or KNOW THE ANSWERS ABOUT YOUR ANCESTORS, each with full good-time loads aboard, but I never heard of a regular procession again.

Well, work has to go on. We couldn't fix to do anything about it, so we had to put up with it. Quite a pack of families moved out of town for privacy and to spare their daughters from getting the new ideas about dress, and so on; but most of us had to stay. Pretty near everyone you met those times looked dazed or scowling—except the "tourists."

I called for Sally one evening about a couple of weeks after the trolley procession. When we came out of the house there was a ding-dong going on down the road. A couple of girls with heads that looked like globes of gilded basketwork were scratching the living daylights out of one another. There was a guy standing by looking mighty like a proud rooster, the rest were whooping things on. We went the other way.

"It just isn't like our town any more," said Sally. "Our homes aren't our homes any more. Why can't they go away and leave us in peace, damn them! I hate them!"

But outside the park we saw one little chrysanthemum-head sitting on apparently nothing at all, and crying her heart out. Sally softened a little.

"Maybe they are human," she said. "But why do they have to turn our town into a darn amusement park?"

We found a bench and sat on it, looking at the sunset. I wanted to get her away out of it.

"It'd be grand to be off up in the hills now," I said.

"It'd be lovely, Jerry." She sighed.

I took her hand, and she didn't pull it away.

"Sally, darling—" I began.

But before I could get any further, two tourists, a man and a girl, came to anchor in front of us. I was angry. You might see the platforms anywhere, but walking tourists didn't find much to interest them in the park as a rule. These two did, though. They stood staring at Sally. She took her hand out of mine. They conferred. The man unfolded a piece of paper he was carrying. They looked at the paper, then at Sally, and then back. It was too much to ignore. I got up and walked through them to see what the paper was. There I had a surprise. It was the Center City News. Obviously a very ancient copy indeed. It was badly browned and tattered at the edges, and to keep it from falling to bits entirely it had been mounted inside some thin, transparent plastic. I looked where they were looking—and Sally's face stared back at me from a smiling photograph. She had her arms spread wide, and a baby in the crook of each. I'd just time to see the headline: "Twins for Inventor's Wife," when they folded up the paper and made off along the path running. I guessed they were hot on the trail to claim one of their infernal prizes—and I hoped it poisoned them.

I went back and sat down again beside Sally. That picture had kind of spoiled things. I'd never invented anything more than an excuse in my life—and I had to do that again right now to avoid telling her what I'd seen.

We sat on a while.

A platform went by labelled:

PAINLESS EDUCATION—
GET CULTURE IN COMFORT

"Maybe it's time we moved," I said.

"Yes," said Sally.

I was wishing I'd seen the date on that paper.

"You don't," I asked casually as we walked, "you don't happen to know any guy that invents things?"

"No," said Sally.

That was something, anyway. . .

NEXT DAY found indignation right up the scale again, with everybody complaining to the police, the mayor, Congress, even the President. But no matter how many and how influential the tops that were blowing, nothing was getting done about it. There were schemes, of course. Jimmy had one: it had to do with either ultra-high or infra-low frequencies which were going to shake the projections of the tourists to bits. Maybe there was something in it, and something on those lines might have been worked out sometime, but right then it wasn't getting any place. It's darned difficult to know what you *can* do about something which is virtually a movie portrait in three dimensions—except find some way of cutting its transmission. All its functions are going on not where you see it, but in the place where its origin is. So how do you get at it? What you are actually seeing doesn't feel, doesn't act, doesn't breathe, doesn't sleep, doesn't—

And at that point I had my idea. It struck me all of a heap—so simple. I grabbed my hat and took myself around to the Mayor's office.

After their daily processions of threateners and screwballs they were wary at first, but then interested. We made a test, then we went to work.

All the next two days the gear came rolling into town. When we were ready we had batteries of Klieg lights, beacon lights, all kinds of lights rigged up on trucks, and we had all the searchlights that the Army, the Navy and the airport people would lend us set strategically round town. We brought in a special consignment of very dark glasses for the citizens, and served them out to all comers. Then we got busy.

Whenever a platform showed, we opened up on it with all the blaze we could bring to bear. We poured all the concentrated glare on them that we could. The people on board covered their eyes and the platform slid to cover. We couldn't reach them inside buildings, but the moment they showed outside again we were on them. After a day of it the tourists started showing up in dark glasses too, but if they were strong enough to dim off those lights they just dimmed everything else clean out.

We kept right on at it, working in shifts day and night—and in a bit we began to see results. No wonder. It couldn't have been a lot of fun having your eyeballs fried at $10.00 a fry. After three days of it, trade fell off badly for Pawley's Peekholes. Evidently the customers wanted to see something more than the inside of a few buildings and an almighty searing glare everywhere outside. And at the end of five days it was pretty well over. . . At least, we say it was over. Jimmy maintains otherwise. According to him, all they did, probably, was to modify out the visibility factor, and it's likely they're still peeking around just the same right now—in Center City and other places. Maybe he's right; maybe that guy Pawley, whoever he is or will be, has got a chain of Fun-Fairs all around the world and all through history operating right now. We wouldn't know—and, as long as he keeps 'em out of sight, we wouldn't care a lot. There's a lot in that old adage: out of sight, out of mind. . .

When we could see we'd got it all tied up I took time to call on Sally. She was looking as lovely as ever.

"Hullo, Jerry," she said. "I've just been reading about you in the paper. I think it's wonderful."

"Nothing so wonderful. Just that I happened to get an idea," I said modestly.

"But it was. It was a wonderful invention."

"Well, it worked, but I'd hardly call it an—" I broke off. "Did you say 'invention?' " I asked.

"Why, of course!"

"Then that would make me an inventor?"

"Why, yes, Jerry. . ." She looked puzzled.

I took a deep breath.

"Sally, darling, there's something I've been trying to say to you for quite a while. . ."

SHE-DUN-IT

Old as history is the canine enigma. Sweet, lovable, clumsy Fido. Is his mischief as innocent as cracked up to be? Consider the threat: every dog has his day. Man's best friend, yes . . . but also bloodhound. And can the mutt be trusted with feminine secrets? This question Mr. Weyl discusses with exceptional authority. An expert in such matters, he is author of Treason, last year's widely acclaimed history of betrayal in America.

BLOOD will tell

NATHANIEL WEYL

If chilled love leads to murder—what does chilled blood lead to? The answer lay with Linda's husband!

As soon as they turned off Canal Street, Robespierre knew where she was going. The car edged through narrow, dingy streets, making frequent turns. Linda's eyes were on the mirror, studying the cars behind. She continued to zigzag until she was certain nobody was following her.

She parked the car in the alley that they had used before, leaving it deep enough inside so that people passing on the street couldn't read the license number. Glenn lived on the street into which the alley gave. Linda walked tentatively into the bright, swarming street, still afraid of being followed. She stopped at a second-hand store which had meerschaum pipes in the window. Behind the meerschaums there was a mirror with a too ornate, gold-leafed frame that leaned lopsided in the display window. Through the mirror, she could command a view of the pedestrians on the street.

When sure that nobody was there who might recognize her, Linda walked quickly to his apartment house. Inside the vestibule she was quite protected from the eyes of the street by the double doors with their frosted glass windows. When she rang Glenn's bell, a spot of dust stained her finger. For a minute they waited, then, when the buzzer clicked, walked up the two flights of unlighted stairs on the shredded, once crimson, carpet.

Glenn opened the door. Although braced by the doorknob and the mantelpiece, his heavy body swayed. His eyes were glazed and his lower lip slack.

She and Robespierre went into the room, which was seething with disorder, and Linda sat down on the sofa. There was a half-empty gin bottle on the floor. The torn shades were down, barring the brilliant afternoon sunlight. The place smelled of turpentine.

"I came after all," Linda said unnecessarily. "I don't know why. Because it's all over and there isn't anything more to say about it." She looked around the room: "So you got potted?"

"What did you expect me to do?" Glenn poured some gin into the cup and took the cup to the faucet. The water came out with a rush, spilling most of the gin down the drain. He went back unsteadily to the bottle and poured a larger drink. This time he was careful with the faucet and didn't spill any liquor. He did all this very slowly, his face screwed up and concentrated on what he was doing. He came back and offered Linda the drink, but she shook her head. Glenn then noticed that his hand was trembling. He took the cup between both hands and drank.

"You said over the phone you didn't want to live without me. You were going to shoot yourself. So instead you get drunk. You know, that's so typical."

Glenn got up and went to the easel. He tore off the cloth dramatically.

"Your portrait is finished," he said. "You can take it home with you."

Of course the portrait was not finished. He had grasped the character of her face in a few sure strokes and then had been too lazy to create the depth and shadows. Linda stared at the painting. What he had done since her last visit was to paint a jagged red line from one corner of the canvas to the other—a line which slashed through her neck.

"That was a childish thing to do," she said, not even trying to hide her contempt. "Why it's like a voodoo witch sticking pins in a wax doll. . . Really, there just isn't anything we have to say to each other. Whatever we once had in common any man can have with any woman and. . ."

"Yes?"

"I am ashamed of having had it with you."

Glenn moved quickly toward the door and intercepted her. His heavy hands with the splashes of dark hair on their backs took her shoulders firmly. The hands moved like tortoises over her body. Although he was too drunk to hold her the way a man should, she felt her knees going weak again. Linda suddenly shook him off.

"I don't want it," she said. "I really don't."

"What *do* you want?"

She looked lost for a moment. Of course, that was just the trouble. If one really knew what one wanted, this sort of thing couldn't happen.

"You're not walking out of that door yet," Glenn said. "We've got to talk. You can't leave me like this. You see I would be absolutely alone, Linda. Don't you understand that?"

"There are other women. The world is full of women."

"Nobody else would ever be any good for me—not after you." Glenn was moving back onto firmer terrain now, Linda thought. The role of the tragic suicide-to-be hadn't quite come off. So he would try charm. She remembered the charm from the other times and shuddered slightly. She went back to the couch and sat down, but didn't take her gloves off.

Glenn poured the cup full of gin and drank half of it in one gulp. She saw that he was building up courage for some purpose and she felt uneasy about it.

"I may be weak," Glenn said with dignity, "but I am also an artist."

"Oh, no—you're not! You have a flair, that's all. Just a flair. You don't have discipline and really you don't have much to say."

"I am an artist," Glenn repeated. "And together we could do anything. If you walk out on me now, I will be back in the alcoholic ward."

"I thought you were going to shoot yourself?"

He took the Walther automatic from the dresser drawer and tossed it from one hand to the other. The gun fell on the floor. He made a motion to pick it up, then decided it wasn't worth the effort.

"The gun is loaded," Glenn said. "All I have to do is take it off safety, point it at the top of my head and pull the trigger." He paused dramatically. "But I don't think I want to. Are you really walking out on me, Linda?"

She laughed. Glenn finished the drink of straight gin, taking it like medicine. In about a quarter of an hour, Linda calculated, he would lose consciousness.

Glenn smiled at her in his crooked way:

"Like to buy one of my paintings, Linda?"

"Are you insane? How would I explain that to Arthur?"

"Store it somewhere. Wait till I am dead and famous. Make money off my corpse when I am dead and famous, Linda. Right now, right at this minute, you can have any canvas in the place for five thousand bucks."

"What are you really trying to say, Glenn?"

"Still rather have you, you understand. But you say I can't. . . And I have to live, Linda. It isn't blackmail, you see. No gentleman ever blackmails. Some day those paintings are going to be priceless, worth priceless money, if you follow me."

"The man's crazy," Linda said to Robespierre. "Come along. We're getting out of here."

"Photographs," Glenn said. "Took photographs while you were sleeping. Did it because I love you so much." His voice broke and she saw to her disgust that he was giggling. He took some prints from his vest pocket and handed them to her. "Hate to do this, you understand. I am a gentleman. No hard feelings, I hope."

By now Glenn was too drunk to see that she was really angry. The blood had left her face and all her muscles were weak. When she had silent rages like this one, Linda was always afraid she would lose control, would do something irrevocable.

She sat stiffly on the edge of the couch, smoking. She was careful not to take her gloves off. She wondered where the negatives were. All she had to do was wait until he passed out, then take the negatives and the prints and walk out the door. She would blot him out of her mind. This would be something in her life that had never happened.

Now he was mumbling that he loved her so much he couldn't live without her. His shirt had sprung a button and she noticed how fat and dead-white his belly was. She thought of something washed up dead on a beach. How disgusting he was when one really thought about it.

It wasn't only the pictures. Sooner or later Glenn would talk. Talk to someone about her—about them. This idea came to her now with great force and clarity. She knew now that he would go from one drunken bout to the next and that sooner or later his tongue would start wagging.

Linda picked up the gun between gloved fingers and released the safety catch. Gently, she put the automatic between his limp fingers and guided his hand toward his head.

Holding his wrist, she waited until the elevated train roared past the window and then said: "Squeeze it, darling."

She helped, of course. Strangely enough, it made very little noise. But what surprised her was the amount of blood. She hadn't dreamed that a man could bleed that much. The bullet must have severed a neck artery.

She moved away from the couch the minute the gun went off. Studying herself in the mirror, Linda saw that there was no blood on her dress, none at all. She swept up the prints from the table and then found the negatives under a ball of dirty handkerchiefs and shirts in the dresser. She put the prints and negatives in her handbag. She even remembered to take the cigarette butts with the lipstick rings on them.

Thank God she hadn't written him letters. Nothing of that sort to worry about.

"Come, Robespierre." As they reached the door, she remembered the canvas. A rotten painting, but at the same a dangerously good likeness. With his palette knife, she cut the canvas from its frame. This took three or four minutes. Then she wrapped the canvas in an old newspaper and left with Robespierre.

Robespierre thought it was good riddance. He had never cared for Glenn, largely because there had been an unpleasant smell to the fellow. He walked happily with Linda to the car, waiting patiently while she dropped the cigarette butts in a trash can.

They drove out to the Palisades and walked in the woods. When she found a secluded spot, Linda emptied a can of lighter fluid on the canvas and film and watched them burn to ashes.

She had some moments of fear, but they passed. There was really nothing to worry about. She had worn gloves all the time. Therefore there couldn't be any fingerprints. Besides, he had squeezed the gun himself. The police would see at once that it was suicide.

It had been quite horrid, Linda thought as she drove up the gravel drive of their home in Westchester. Exciting while it lasted, frightfully exciting, but fundamentally so repugnant and sordid. One didn't like to say that sort of thing, but really it was better for Glenn this way. Being dead, that is. Now he could be at peace and he wouldn't have those frightful drunken spells and scream in his room about the colorless, transparent animals. Yes, actually it had been a kindness.

Dear Arthur was standing framed in the front door waiting for her. He seemed so comforting, so solid and kind, that her heart went out to him. She felt a warm glow of satisfaction at having broken with Glenn in a way that couldn't conceivably cause Arthur any pain. She ran to meet her husband and kissed him ardently.

Arthur wiped his mouth with his handkerchief. They went into the living room with Robespierre following. Arthur poured the old-fashioneds.

"There's been intriguing news over the radio," he remarked. "That young painting fellow, Glenn Corrigan, the one you disliked so much. Well, the top of his head has been blown off." When she remained silent, Arthur added: "I thought the Corrigan tidbit would interest you, darling. After all, you *did* dislike him so. I rather thought the news might give you pleasure, in a way."

"He did seem to be the suicidal type," Linda said.

"Suicide? I hardly think so. You see there were paw prints in the dead man's blood. A remarkable quadruped. He apparently left the room after the artist fellow had been killed and then closed the door behind him."

Linda knew she mustn't look. She concentrated on her drink, but slowly, as if by a magnet, her eyes were drawn toward Robespierre, who was curled up in his favorite chair, licking the brown patches staining his paws. A glance at Arthur's cold face told her that he not only knew about Glenn, but probably had always known. He sat there withdrawn, perched on the edge of the big chair, a small, prim, middle-aged man whom she had wounded and who now hated her. He lifted the telephone.

"I want a policeman," he said.

MYSTERY

Like the hurricane, she was wickedly beautiful — and left a trail of wreckage

the nightmare face

WALTER SNOW

HE FOUND ME in the Bahama Bar. The humid air was blue with cigarette haze. When the battered street door gaped open, the tailwinds of the dying hurricane howled with louder weirdness across the shambles of the nearby Key West turtle crawls. Slapped loose the pilings in that stockyard of the sea, banged the torn tin roof of the cannery, ripped through rattling debris. The assembled turtle slaughterers, packers and fishermen shuddered, gulped at straight drinks. I was drinking rum.

Then suddenly he stood beside me, hunching forward as if still fighting off the lashing storm.

Shaking a dripping yellow slicker, he seemed a small, insignificant *conch,* a shrunken five-feet-six, a shriveled 130-odd pounds. I towered over him, a lanky beanpole, a smarter man, a respected well-known man. But Leander Jones was wiry like a hound, weather-toughened like an alligator. A scowl darkened the ruddy face which contrasted so strongly with white hair and tobacco-stained, scraggly moustache. Steel eyes glinted.

Obviously, "Judge" Leander Jones was on a scent. He was a virtual one-man homicide squad for a thousand Florida Keys—most active among

. . . about the author

Walter Snow's father, once a Connecticut sheriff, may have inspired the peace officer in this powerful story—though several persons swear to having met an actual counterpart of Judge Leander down among the Florida Keys. As for Walter, he's worked as bobbin boy, scene shifter, infantryman, and reporter for the Brooklyn Eagle *and* New York Post, *managing in between to live in Havana, Key West and Provincetown. A director of Mystery Writers of America, his work has adorned more than 30 magazines.* The Nightmare Face *will shortly appear in* Murder by Experts *(second series) to be published by Random House.*

the Deputy Sheriffs, Monroe County Coroner and Justice of the Peace representing law here in Key West.

"A gal friend of ours has been murdered," he said.

The raised glass of rum sloshed over, trickled down my chin like ice water.

"Want you to come to Barracuda Key," said the icy tone of command.

He didn't mention the name. Only one scarlet flower, more exotic than hibiscus, had ever bloomed on that tiny, desolate key. The thought of her had always been enough to send my pulses rocketing. Mrs. Jeff Crane. Carlotta of the silky, raven hair. The alluring teaser. The faithless tramp. . . .

The blue cigarette haze lifts. Again I see her for the first time, prancing around as a barefoot bartender in a Duval Street dump. I confide to my guide and fishing pal, Leander Jones, that she's a hussy destined for horsewhipping. The Judge nods grimly, "Thought so once." Carlotta flirts indiscriminately with eager sailors, pats their cheeks, blows them kisses. When they get too fresh she brandishes a baseball bat prankishly. It's an act that keeps the bar crowded when the fleet is in. Brazenly, Carlotta sasses all her customers: "You're stingy tippers. Me, I want a man with money."

The way she swings scantily clad hips and twinkles smoky, mischievous eyes makes them like it. Intrigues even Leander and myself. She seems a poor man's *femme fatale,* a waterfront Mata Hari, a Cracker Cleopatra.

Carlotta had drifted down from the cattle bogs of the mainland a few months before I'd come to Key West. Got her first job as waitress at the Crawfish Pot. Leander, a widower, wanted to run her out of town. Then he had taken to dining out on seafood as if he were a tourist and not the best fisherman and chef on the keys. He bought her a tiny wristwatch studded with diamonds, a 14-karat bracelet, a string of seed pearls, but she only laughed:

"You're too poor and too tough! You'll live too long. I want a rich old man who'll kick the bucket soon."

To encounter wider opportunities, Carlotta had shifted from waitress to barefoot bartender. Had attained half her goal as Mrs. Jeff Crane.

Have you seen my pictures of her? Not a classic beauty, just a saucy vixen of a Cracker gal. Face a bit too long, seductive figure a shade buxom; but I, Bruce Wallace, National Academy member, a Carnegie Prize winner represented in twenty museums, painted her a dozen times for posing fees that mounted with each new canvas. My Carnegie Prize portrait shows her as a ragged *conch* standing beside an overturned crawfish boat—barefooted, her dress in tatters, her face smudged but with an electric quality, an element appeal that sets a man afire. . .

The blue haze in the bar closed me in again. I wanted another tall glass of rum: the "Southernmost Hangover," but Judge Jones' dry voice made me abruptly forget thirst.

"I can't prove Carlotta was murdered. You, as an artist, might help me get a confession."

In the steel eyes glinted an unexpected friendliness, a plea for cooperation. Judge Leander Jones was still my pal. In a daze, I followed him to his car, listened to the dry voice drone on about discovering the crime while visiting fishing camps up the keys to check on possible storm casualties.

Cold rain sheeted our windshield, the tailwinds were still bending dwarf cabbage palms, when we turned into the marl side road running off the Overseas Highway.

"There's Jeff now," said Leander.

Pelting rain obscured my view. At first I saw only a low stone building, squatting beside a clump of bent mangroves on the edge of the Atlantic. The Barracuda Key Fishing Lodge seemingly stood intact. But an ancient wooden boatshed, which once nestled against the western side of the stone fortress, was a tangled mess of debris. A few leaning piles, stretching into the churning ocean, were all that remained of the dock.

Hunched on the stoop, a grizzled patriarch hid eyes and face in gnarled hands. With the rain still slanting in from the Atlantic, he was drenched to the skin. But old Jeff Crane seemed oblivious to the grinding of brakes, the skidding tires on the crushed coral road.

"Where's Doc Healy?" said Leander.

The old fisherman lowered bony hands, looked up strangely. His hatchet face was an overgrown jungle of whiskers; bushy gray hair hung over the ears and the crumpled, dirty shirt-collar. Under shaggy fog-gray brows, rheumy eyes were swelled, almost closed by huge cataracts.

"Who's that?" he asked, blinking.

"It's Leander. How's the missus?"

"She went away," said old Jeff in a sepulchral voice. "They finally drove away together. The fury of the Lord should have struck them down in their sin. But in the storm, in the righteous anger of the Almighty, the lights went out for me forever. It was my punishment because I tolerated their sin."

The ravings of this half-cracked miser steadied my nerves. All that was needed now was to prove that old Jeff was lying about being blind. Or had he really been stricken?

Nervously, I pulled out a cigarette, struck my lighter. It was king-size, a miniature blowtorch to withstand high winds. As the wick flared, Jeff jerked his head around.

"You saw that!" I shouted. "You're bluffing."

"I heard it."

Just then the door opened. Dr. Healy, the Coroner's physician, an easy-going potbelly, stepped out of the house followed by a swarthy State highway cop, Jose Gonzales. Gonzales remained with old Jeff; the Judge and the Doc lead me down towards the waterfront. I hated to think of seeing Carlotta again.

Into the rear basement of the stone lodge jutted a garage-type boathouse. The massive storm door, now partly open, showed a gaping knot-hole. Inside, two skiffs stretched secure on racks; a twenty-foot powerboat rested in a few inches of water. The circumference of the knot-hole was rough with hacked marks, circled by dozens of irregular indentations.

"An auto jack or heavy wrench knocked in that knot," said the Judge, grimly. "The hurricane couldn't make those marks. Two people, locked out in the storm, tried desperately to get into this secure boathouse. Look at them!"

Enough debris had been cleared away to bare the bloated remains of two storm-battered bodies—more horrible than I had dreamed. They lay huddling against the stone foundation of the lodge. Carlotta didn't seem mutilated in front; her head was bashed in from the rear. With raven hair clotted by blood and a corpse's pallor on the once mischievous face. With dead, glassy eyes, she no longer looked desirable. She looked ruthless and hard.

The other victim I recognized as Bill Adams, a curly-headed ne'er-do-well, hired last winter to pilot the sports fishermen who had been coming for years to this camp and had made it a gold mine. Bill's skull was smashed. His once handsome Roman nose had been pounded flat. Carlotta had gone crazy over this good-looking rascal, flaunted him everywhere, dropped her other men. All Key West half-expected that some day old Jeff might have a fatal accident and that Bill Adams would marry the heiress. Now the picture was reversed. I shuddered and turned away.

"How can you prove," asked Dr. Healy, "that this wasn't accidental homicide from the hurricane? Maybe the old codger didn't get potted on Stock Island, didn't leave his car there and get somebody else to drive him home. Or maybe he deliberately left his car there to bar escape. But can you prove that Jeff locked Carlotta and Bill outside during the fury of the storm? Can you prove that Carlotta and Bill pounded on the door, pleaded? Old Jeff insists he heard nothing. The hurricane could drown out even a sledge-hammer. For four infernal hours the winds raged up to 165 miles an hour. Here, on this exposed beach, how could anything live through that?"

"He's bluffing blindness," protested Leander Jones.

"Carlotta drove him to town just this week to see me about his eyes," said the Doc. "Of course he might have been acting cagey but he was at least three-quarters blind. Cataracts are a delicate operation. I recommended a good ophthalmologist in Miami."

"This week, huh. When?"

"Monday, I think. I can look it up."

"That was one day before the hurricane. When it was raining torrents. When he knew the big storm was coming."

"By the blankety-blank, Leander! Are you implying that he used me as an alibi?"

The Judge turned away with a contemptuous snort, told me to relieve Gonzales as Jeff's guard, send the highway cop to him.

Jeff was clumping around the big lodge like a clumsy grizzly bear. He knocked over a straight chair, almost went headlong into the empty fireplace. I made him sit down on a couch, walked over to the mantelpiece and looked around. As an artist, I was peeved at the absence of pictures in this huge room. The knotty pine walls were virtually bare. Above the fireplace, an ideal spot for a huge painting, dangled a tiny calendar with a "September Morn" nude. Irritated, I snatched down the mildly salacious calendar, held it to my lighter and tossed it into the cold hearth. Jeff didn't move or blink. Was he being "cagey?" In a few moments, Judge Jones' dry voice called out.

"Hey, Bruce! Bring Jeff here!"

Stretched out on the sand was the storm-battered body of Carlotta, her wet tresses looking like writhing, black snakes. Just below her feet lay Bill Adams' corpse. The Doc, the Judge and Gonzales were lined up in back of this weird barrier.

"Come here, Bruce," commanded the Doc, sweeping his arm down across Carlotta's corpse.

With a queasy sensation in the pit of my stomach, I walked in a straight line, carefully stepped over the mangled body to reach the three other witnesses. Felt relieved only when I closed my eyes.

"You too, Jeff. Come here a minute."

"Well. . . somebody give me a hand!"

"Help him, Bruce," said the Doc.

"I'm right here, Jeff. Here you go," I said, without moving.

Jeff paused a moment, reached out bony arms, felt nothing. Then he started staggering forward. He edged up towards the high ground, in the direction just above Carlotta's head.

"You there?" asked Jeff.

"Right here!" I called from Carlotta's feet.

Jeff shifted direction, suddenly kicked into Carlotta's shoulder. Tripping, he plunged sideways, falling directly on top of the cold, stiff body.

Now he was on his knees, rubbing the lifeless hands.

"Are you hurt, Carlotta? Speak, Carlotta. I forgive you everything."

"Bet you'd hate to testify to this scene in court," said Dr. Healy, lowering his voice and leading us out of range of Jeff's hearing. "Jeff's blindness would win any jury's sympathy. All local jurors know that weird terrors happen in a hurricane. Besides believing in the unwritten law, they'd think Jeff has only a year or two to live, anyway."

"But he locked 'em outside!"

"The question is can you prove it?"

"That's where Bruce comes in," said Leander Jones. "How long d'you think a killer can stare at the faces of his murder victims?"

An icicle started crawling up my spine. Biting my lower lip, I silenced chattering teeth. With the will power of an aggressive man, the will power that had made me persist while a thousand would-be artists fell by the wayside of rejections, I controlled trembling hands.

"We'll take Jeff down to the courthouse for questioning," explained the Judge relentlessly. "We'll give Bruce time to paint death portraits of Carlotta and Bill Adams over the mantelpiece. If Jeff is faking blindness, he won't dare to cover them up. We'll drop around every other day to inspect the pictures. If he lives with the dead faces long enough, if he's haunted by them. . .well. . . "

I awoke still seeing staring eyes; glassy dead eyes. Hearing thunder. Had the new hurricane struck? Groggily I reached for the chain of the bedside reading lamp. There was a dull click; the room remained in inky blackness. I hunched forward on one elbow, gasped.

Remembered flopping on the bed fully dressed after taking a sleeping pill.

Outside the rains whipped down, the winds howled and something banged furiously. It could not be a storm shutter: all had been double-hooked from the inside, everything had been battened down. But the racket continued—pound, bang, crash—each a blow against my aching head. I listened. Not yet were the winds whistling, frantically straining the hurricane cables attached to the four cornerposts of the roof.

"Hey, Bruce, open up!"

That nasal, too familiar voice set my teeth chattering. So it was the Judge banging! Biting my upper lip, I wondered if I could pretend absence. For months Leander Jones had been a genial old salt, a good crony who had shown me the wizardry of tarpon fishing. On rainy days I had often dropped in at the Monroe County Courthouse, near the President's winter white house, for a friendly poker session. Now he was the last man I wanted to see.

Slowly I arose on rubbery legs, lurched to the door, unlocked it. A gust of wind, a sheet of cold rain and the wiry *conch* blew in.

"Damn it, Bruce, I'm soaked. Gotta candle? The power went off twenty minutes ago. It seems like midnight but it's 9 a. m."

Fumbling with a match, I noticed the steely glint in the Judge's deep sunken eyes. The flicker of the candle illuminated a large studio with a rumpled bed and in one corner a heavy easel. The Judge squinted at the work in progress, the big canvas on the easel. It was to be a vivid scene of uprooted palms and a wrecked crawfish boat on the beach. Curiously the Judge stepped over to a stack of canvases turned to the wall. He took out a portrait of Carlotta as a laughing vixen, placed it on the easel, studied it. Then he lifted out another, stared . . .

"We gotta go on a trip before the big blow strikes."

"I'm sorry, Leander. I'm staying here. Maybe it's this new hurricane roaring across Cuba now, headed straight for us. Maybe I'm like your average juror, who believes in the unwritten law. It hit me like a thunderbolt yesterday. I was having a quick one in the Bahama Bar when I saw old Jeff Crane. He was in town, stacking up groceries to last through the new storm."

"And you thought him innocent?"

"He's an old, broken man."

"Bruce, I'm on the verge of cracking this case. Come out with me this one more time. You need rain in the face, a drive to sober up."

Gonzales was outside in a car, drove it to Barracuda Key. The Judge fingered lips for silence as we entered the isolated lodge.

Leaning against the mantelpiece, old Jeff Crane was staring up at the nightmarish portraits I had painted. Fascinated, hypnotized by the gruesome corpse-like faces, the accusing dead eyes. Gonzales took out handcuffs, clanked them together.

"Look!" I cried. "The old codger can see."

"Yes," said Leander Jones. "Old Jeff finally admitted this morning that he had pretended blindness—for fear he'd be accused."

The Judge's voice came from behind me. Bony hands seized my wrists. Gonzales stepped up. Steel clinked. The two yanked me down into a straight-backed chair, tied me facing the death portraits.

"Is this a joke?" I asked, shaking. "Are you crazy?"

They lit two hurricane lamps, placed one on each side of the mantelpiece. Left me there, tied and handcuffed, as the wind whistled eerily that the new storm was striking. Left me staring at the mutilated man and the hussy with long raven hair and dead, glassy eyes. "How long," the Judge had asked, "d'you think a killer can stare at the faces of his murder victims?"

With the wild winds whining, with gigantic billows savagely sloshing against the stone lodge, my mounting panic almost developed into hysteria as I yelled that I was innocent, that I was a famous artist.

Then reason returned, launched a counter-attack, argued that if this third-degree stunt were mere bluff, I could win out.

Methodically I checked details for a possible slip-up. How could they prove that I, Bruce Wallace, N.A., had gone mad from loneliness and jealousy because a tramp like Carlotta would no longer come to my studio, would only see the worthless Bill Adams? The fact that they expected my own pictures to break me down demonstrated that there was no proof. Was there a hint, a tiny blunder? Let's see. On the afternoon before the first storm I had found old Jeff in the Stock Island Bar, just north of Key West. He was already so drunk that he didn't see me. I had sleeping tablets in my pocket, slipped three or four into his liquor. Old Jeff thought he was sick, staggered outside, collapsed. He didn't know I drove him home unconscious.

I'm not a murderer. I had no premeditated plan then, just hoped for an opportunity to see Carlotta alone. Probably I hoped just as much for a chance to encounter Bill Adams alone, wanted to beat him up. But the two lovers were in the shed just outside the basement boathouse. They were embracing, cooing . . . It seemed so perfect—murder with a blunt instrument on the eve of the hurricane. A few clues arranged to point at the old man who wouldn't be convicted.

It *was* perfect. I used a club of palmetto on them, a wrench on the knot-hole. Yet now I was tied to a chair, facing those accusing eyes while the storm reached its maniacal climax. Did they think I would flinch from horror?

Suddenly the winds ceased abruptly, as if a celestial electric current had been switched off. An ominous silence descended as the dead center, the hole in the hurricane doughnut, passed over. The unknown, the mystery of a possible mistake, was a scalpel probing my brain. My mind raced around in an endless zigzag. Faster and faster. The eerie silence was maddening. Once more it was the ghastly moment after murder. Utter loneliness, barren desolation. Suddenly a voice punctured the stillness like pistol shots.

"Open your eyes," commanded Leander Jones. "The proof is there. Your own painting of that nightmare face!"

In the deathly silence I stared with widened eyes, understood that my friend, my fishing pal, wasn't bluffing. He would keep me, if necessary, tied up for endless hours until the portrait over the mantel, the sounds or silences of the storm, something, broke me.

"Take me away," I begged. "But when did you suspect?"

"I didn't for two weeks," said a hoarse, strained voice. "Old Jeff unknowingly gave me the idea this morning. Remarked that your death portrait didn't show Carlotta as 'purty' as she was. It struck me like lightning that I was the half-blind one. I rushed to look at your earlier alluring Carlottas. In your final painting here, is she a woman desired, loved even in death? Look at those hard lines, the mouth of a vicious trollop. It proclaims that you hated enough to kill her!"

He lowered his tired head, trembled at the new winds sobbing through the lonely palms and palmettoes. My friend had performed his duty.

THOMAS GILCHRIST

SURVIVAL

Assorted semi-simians and missing links, banding together against the elements, initiated the cooperations we call civilization. But when the elements rebel—or when man's disloyalty

WALKABOUT stirred to awareness of a splash but he did not at once look over the side. He was immediately conscious of his bones, cramped as they were in the narrow bow of the dinghy, and he moved to give them some freedom. Upon opening his eyes the first thing he saw was a wavering, undulating mass of black in the stern sheets; and when, presently, his sick eyes focused and the mass steadied and resolved itself, the preacher remembered it was the Kanaka. Bu squatted with his elbow in one hand and his chin in the other, dark, silent and primitive as the elements, like something the formidable night itself had left behind.

The other white man, Murdoch, straddled the 'midships thwart, to one side, but Walkabout did not look at him. He knew already that Murdoch was sneering. He knew also that the little swirl alongside, the little subsiding swirl that alone broke the vast mirror of the sea, accounted for the fourth man.

Behind the Kanaka a bar of light was breaking above the horizon. It changed swiftly to riotous orange and red and green. A planet was snuffed out and the sun, blood-red and immense, lifted quickly and with purpose out of the sea, blazed suddenly and dissipated the short-lived glory of the Pacific dawn. And the interminable night gave way at last to another and more interminable day.

Walkabout drew himself upright, drew his fingers outwards across his eyes and down over his brine-encrusted beard. He looked up again

Ancient as the islands were these Kanaka mysteries. Would they prevail against trackless ocean—and the evil white man?

to man destroys the union—then civilization may fail, including its precious science. Then the savage walk triumphant! Here's the whole story in, precisely, a nutshell.

and when he spoke it was not to Murdoch.

"What happened, Bu?"

The Kanaka looked up and his cave of a mouth opened and his eyes glittered redly but he did not speak.

"What happen *imatung* Grayson?" Walkabout tried again, though he had been unable to find a common dialect with this native.

The dinghy lay perfectly still, there was not a whisper of a breeze, not a ripple on the water now. The sun was already scorching their bodies; a small white-metal buckle lying on a thwart reflected its brilliance. It was Murdoch who answered at last, his voice thick with fear and malice:

"What the hell do you think, preacher? He died, of course. So we saved you a job. We threw him over." He paused. He was panting already with the effort of speech. "I told you we should have saved his water ration," he shouted. "He'd have died anyway."

"As we shall ourselves, no doubt," the preacher told him placidly. "Very soon."

Murdoch looked at the old man insanely, then back at the Kanaka. "Get up!" Murdoch shouted. "Get up and do something, you bloody scavenger! What d'you think I hired you for? Christ!"

Walkabout watched through half-closed eyes. Bu grinned uncomprehendingly and the grin made a hole in his face like a pit. His huge tongue lolled between powerful white teeth and a chuckle came across the boat. Walkabout saw that Murdoch was shivering now, shivering and sweating in the growing heat; and he knew Murdoch was remembering that men still ate their kind.

Murdoch turned to Walkabout again, quickly, frightened. There were heavy pouches under Murdoch's eyes. Lines ran from his nose to the sides of his sun-blistered lips, lines made darker by a week's growth of beard. His face, that had been naturally pale, was now aflame like his shock of hair and his stocky legs. His thick hands trembled on his knees. He was clad only in shorts and a singlet.

"Christ!" he breathed again.

Walkabout inclined his head. "You may well call upon Him," he said.

"Upon who?" Murdoch snarled. "God?" He looked at the Kanaka again and he laughed on a rising note of hysteria. "Yes—God and this bloody savage!" he shouted. "How long do you think it'll be, preacher?"

Walkabout closed smarting eyes, opened them again to the intolerable glare of the sun.

"Depends on your faith, Murdoch," he said. "Your faith in God—or maybe in this bloody savage, as you call him." His long nose twitched again. He hove himself up and supported his body with his elbows on the gunnel and a malicious note was in his voice when he spoke again. "He won't eat you—yet—if that's what you're afraid of," he said. "It's your red hair—and ginger beard—Murdoch. I fancy he'll want to let your beard grow some more."

Murdoch was holding his breath. He expelled it now.

"It's an oddity in the Islands, a ginger head," the preacher informed him. "The women go nuts over them. They want red-headed babies. The men go crazy over them, too. They have a way of preserving them and hanging them up in their huts. Gives them prestige, a red head."

Murdoch stared at the old man, jaw hanging loose, and Walkabout closed his eyes again. He wished he'd been better known in—and himself know better—the Gilbert and Ellice Islands. He was known in nearly every other group in the South Pacific. He had been wandering about the Islands for as long as most whites could remember, and he was not unaware of his reputation. To the natives he was something of a legend. They had called him Walkabout because of his energetic pacings up and down and around and about when he delivered his sermons. He entertained while he instructed, and in this he was deliberate. To the whites he never denied the remnants of an American accent — confused now with a welter of native dialects, pidgeon English and a smattering of Oxford, lifted for his own amusement from King's Commissioners. Nor did he trouble to deny the rumor that he had once been a 'Frisco pug and playboy. He never bothered to deny or acknowledge anything concerning himself, intent as he was upon hammering home the Word; drawing only when strictly necessary upon his pugilistic prowess.

Hunger tore his insides now and his parched tongue all but choked him, but he had an urgent need for self-expression.

"Consider, Murdoch," he said, "the quaint humor of Destiny, the three complexities of civilization she's thrown together in a twelve-foot dinghy. A month ago—a mere month ago—you were in your stockbroker's office in Sydney. You were manipulating millions in currency, bank presidents probably fawned upon you, thousands depended — once hooked—upon your good will. And then you took your yacht for a cruise and skippered her yourself, since you're a navigator, a yachtmaster—by school standards. But the Pacific—the vast, implacable Pacific—did what it does to most amateurs who don't respect her. She turned your toy of a ship upside down, and now—where are you? A navigator!"

"What's this—a sermon?" Murdoch sneered. "If I had my sextant—"

"If you had your sextant—and your chronometers and almanacs and tables," Walkabout added. "In that case I could reckon our position myself."

The boat stirred and they both looked sharply at the Kanaka. He was paddling with the bailer, spinning the dinghy. He changed the paddle to the other side and the small craft shot ahead and presently they saw a coconut shell alongside. Bu scooped it up, grinning, almost with an air of triumph. He held it aloft and examined it in the manner of a connoisseur.

It was only a half shell and it was without meat. Walkabout closed his eyes again, wearily.

That had been Bu's business, of course, scavenging. After Walkabout had taken passage on the yacht, they had anchored in Tabiteuea, and there Murdoch had first seen the Kanaka: sitting in his dugout against the background of the reef, fishing with a line between his toes, paddling without hurry to pick up a bottle or a can thrown from the yacht.

"By God!" Murdoch had said. "Now there's something for you! There's sheer independence for you! Scavenging the sea by day, sleeping on the earth by night. And propagating the species—"

He had told Walkabout that he thought it would make a good story back in Sydney; and that night in the cabin he had rehearsed it to his guests and dutiful listeners:

"And that's how one part of the so-called human race lives . . . following its instincts like the beasts of the jungle." Murdoch had evidently liked that thought. He had been intrigued by the Kanaka much as he would have been intrigued by an ape. He had hired him as a sort of specimen. . . .

Walkabout felt the dribble of lukewarm water on his chest and he opened his eyes without alarm. Bu was standing over him, naked as the day he was born, and he was wringing out his *lava-lava*. He dipped it in the sea again, his motions so easy that he never disturbed the balance of the frail craft. His muscles rippling under smooth, brown skin, he bathed the old man's legs with the gentle touch of a woman. Like Murdoch, Walkabout had been asleep when the yacht tossed them all into the Pacific, and he was wearing only shorts and a rag of an undershirt.

The old man nodded as Bu turned to Murdoch with the dripping *lava-lava,* and he saw Murdoch cringe. It gave Walkabout an odd sense of betrayal. He experienced a brief surge of anger that no man of God should have permitted himself. Murdoch's mouth opened and closed and Walkabout saw that he was trying to speak but couldn't because the metal buckle had been placed in his mouth. Bu continued his ministrations and when he had finished he retrieved the buckle and gave it to Walkabout to suck. It induced a very small amount of saliva. Then Bu slipped gently overboard.

The sun climbed and smote the white men like the blast from a furnace. There were only bars of shadows directly under the thwarts now. Murdoch had wilted, passed into a stupor. Walkabout himself could hardly stir his bones in the sack of his skin. Pain stabbed him to the marrow when he moved. A formidable emptiness filled his shrunken stomach and his swollen tongue could scarcely taste the metal buckle. It had been a whole week now. He knew that the end was near.

The boat tipped slightly and he opened his eyes again. Bu was climbing back over the stern, using one hand for leverage. His body dripped and glistened as he moved, his eyes shone redly and he breathed a little heavily. In his free hand he held his knife. And then Walkabout was conscious of a sudden flow of saliva to his mouth; for, spitted on the blade, was a little leathery slate-gray fish.

Walkabout's eyes lit as he recognized the fish. The law of chance or, more scientifically, the calculus of probability, had pulled off a miracle. He knew that a shark had contributed that fish; that a shark had been with them for a while and had left, leaving its parasite, *remora,* the sucker fish, attached to the bottom of the boat among the marine growth. And so they would eat. They would eat because a shark had found a surface upon which to scratch itself. It was something of a miracle, but when Bu had carefully removed the eyes and was pounding the fish into a mixture of green weed, he remembered it was the Kanaka who had restrained them from removing and using the weed even when they were crazy with hunger. It was an application of the laws of Nature. It was primitive wisdom transcending scientific knowledge. And Walkabout began to hope again.

Bu fed them a part of the mixture and then gave them the eyes of the fish to suck, for that kept the thirst away. Walkabout remembered this fact only when he experienced it. He remembered long droughts in the Islands when even the landholders had gone fishing because of the eyes. And this reminded him that island communities were divided into two simple groups, the landholders and the fishermen—but once there had been a small class of aristocrats: the navigators of the tribe. They were the really great few, the early Polynesian navigators, who had handed their secrets down only to their sons.

Walkabout raised his head and looked intently at the Kanaka, who was absorbed now in removing the fiber from the coconut shell. But presently he shook his head wearily. Since the coming of the *imatung*—the white man—native craft had died. One only heard vague tales now of those old navigational feats. . . .

He looked again at the immense emptiness of the sky, listened to the profound silence of the universe. The sun was half-meridian, behind him, and his head cast a shadow over his body, relieving it. He fell into an exhausted sleep.

He awoke to the crazy wallow of the dinghy and the inhuman scream, and he lunged instantly at Murdoch. Fire ran through his marrow and blazed before his eyes, but he kept Murdoch from slipping over the side. Bu came over and together they got him to the bottom boards again, where he subsided, face in hands.

"You are right, preacher," he said after a while; and Walkabout knew a moment of relief—until Murdoch continued: "You've had your day. You're beyond love—or don't know it—like the blackfella. I am different. I've got to live. I can't lose her."

Walkabout's still strong teeth showed through his beard in what might have been a smile. It was incredible! On the yacht Murdoch had talked a good deal about Connie, his wife; had passed her photo around—along with those of his automobiles and a complete album showing the magnificent interior of his house. So that this love he talked about was nothing more than pride of possession; but by Murdoch's own standards it was, evidently, something that gave him the right to live, even if others should die. . . . Walkabout heard him speak again, hoarsely.

"We should kill the blackfella!"

For a moment Walkabout couldn't speak. And then he laughed. He laughed until he wondered if he himself were giving way to hysteria, and he stopped abruptly.

In this wreck of a man with insanity flickering in his eyes, he could scarcely recognize the stockbroker. It had taken just a week. The physical deterioration was natural. This was the Kanaka's environment — not theirs. But that with the teaching of two thousand years Murdoch had not acquired any moral fiber—that, to Walkabout, was unpardonable.

"How?" he asked. "He's got the knife. And only he is able to stand."

"That's right!" Murdoch whispered. "He's the only one with a knife. That's right!" He looked up suddenly. "Why d' you suppose he's feeding us, preacher?"

"Why? Isn't that self-evident, Murdoch?" Walkabout ran his fingers down the stickiness of his beard and watched the other carefully. "If you wanted to transport some—beef, say—and you had no means of preserving it *en route,* how would you do it?" he asked. "Take it on the hoof, wouldn't you?"

Murdoch's eyes burned, looking at him. "Christ!" he said.

Walkabout closed his eyes.

When he awoke it was to the gentle fanning of a breeze and the sight of a single cloud in the east. Bu was crouched over his coconut shell, steadily boring holes with the point of his knife. Murdoch straddled the thwart, his mouth not hanging now, his eyes moving from one to the other. Walkabout hove himself upright and scanned the sea. It was rippled, whispering alongside the boat. The immense silence was broken at last. It was as if a verdict had been delivered. He plucked at the undershirt that clung to his suffocating body and let the delicious breeze caress his skin.

"But we're still lost," Murdoch said, as if the other had spoken. "And all that bloody savage can do is sit there and make ornaments! Ornaments out of coconut shells!"

"They also use them in the process of shrinking heads," Walkabout said.

"Shut up!" Murdoch shouted.

"I find it intriguing," Walkabout persisted, "to think of one of God's black children placidly gnawing on the thigh bone of a bank president—or a Sydney stockbroker; and his worldly head decorating the hut of an island chief!"

"Christ!" said Murdoch again, savagely. He stared at the Kanaka. "Yes," he said. "He's making ornaments, all right. I've got some—had some—on the yacht. Ashtrays and things," he chattered.

Walkabout continued to watch Bu through half-closed eyes. The Kanaka was shipping the tiller now. That done, he set a tiny makeshift sail with his *lava-lava* and the boat hook. He moved the tiller with his foot and the dinghy tugged forward. He remained standing, shading his eyes and looking into the setting sun. And when the change of light told Walkabout that the sun had set behind him, he saw Bu sit down again and reach for his coconut shell.

And Walkabout considered, with dawning intelligence. Had he been navigating his old mission-schooner he'd have been taking a bearing of the sun now—an amplitude at sunset—to check his compass. There was no compass here, but there was, he remembered from those old native tales, a relationship between the sunset bearing and the run of the sea and the particular season; and this breeze was the beginning of the south-east trades.

It was, after all, elementary! It was so darned elementary, in fact, that it had escaped the notice of the scientific minds, the educated ego, of his own race! Walkabout marveled and he licked his lips slowly:

"Bu—you sonovagun!"

Bu heard his name and looked up; nodded but said nothing. Walkabout nodded back gently. Murdoch had been watching them both carefully. "There's something between you two! You mamby-pamby parsons and your savages! You suck up to them—ruin them! Letting the race down!"

Walkabout didn't answer, only wondered, suddenly, where the other had found so much new energy. And with that his eyes fell on the after thwart where the remaining rations of fish and weed had been . . .

Oddly, it didn't occur to him to suspect the Kanaka. He turned his head again slowly and looked into the leering face of the other.

"You sonovabitch, Murdoch!" he

said. He returned his attention to Bu. In the twilight, Bu was standing now with the half coconut shell in his hands, and he had filled it with water. It dribbled through the holes that were punched, equi-distant, below the rim. There was a little nick on part of the rim itself. Walkabout followed the direction of his gaze and saw that he was watching the star, *Sirius,* that peered brilliantly over the western horizon. And as *Sirius* set he saw him raise the coconut shell very carefully, so that no water spilled. He turned towards the south and placed his eye to a hole in the shell; and in the southern sky a great, bejewelled cross was hung. . . .

Kaama! It was *Kaama,* the Southern Cross; and the Great Star of *Kaama,* which was *a Crucis* in Walkabout's books. The natives had spoken a good deal—years ago—of the Great Star of *Kaama,* as if it held the secret of life; much as the sun worshippers must have looked upon the sun. Walkabout stared now, forgetting pain and hunger.

It was clear that Bu was taking a meridianal observation of *a Crucis* through the "sights" of his coconut shell! And—of course—the water in the shell, governed by the series of holes, made a perfect horizontal plane —an artificial horizon!

It was utterly preposterous at first! Walkabout ran his fingers over his brow in puzzlement. It was so simple it defied immediate understanding. One needed declinations and right ascensions and a sextant that would measure an altitude. It was impossible otherwise. But it came to him at last. All stars, of course, maintained the same relative position to each other. When, in these latitudes, *Sirius* set, *a Crucis* was, evidently, at its zenith. If a man knew the standard of measurement, he could cut sights in a coconut shell to indicate a given latitude by that star's meridian altitude in relation to the rim. If it showed above the rim, you were south, and if below, north of your standard latitude.

After all, it was only a matter of long and accumulated observation. And what else was science?

Walkabout laughed silently. The impudence of it! The stupendous simplicity of this old miracle, this mystery! He subsided, fearing hysteria again, and he watched as Bu lowered the shell, sat down and leaned on the tiller. The boat came round and as night closed in again they were steering a northerly course by the pointer stars of the Giant Dipper. They indicated the Pole Star, which couldn't be seen in southern latitudes—which the Kanaka could never have seen. But he had set a course by it!

Walkabout laughed again, silently, because he didn't want to appear derisive. There was a wisdom under God transcending mere intelligence if you were ready to accept it. But then he caught his breath. The Kanaka's calculations could only be very rough, of course. Lucky if they were within thirty or forty miles. And at their couple of feet above sea level they wouldn't see an island more than a few miles distant. Walkabout closed his eyes again.

In the morning the sun came up in the old man's face and he knew that Bu was still steering west. He sat by the tiller, not moving, like something carved in mahogany. Murdoch was awake, sitting astride the middle thwart, and his jaw hung loose and only his eyes moved.

"Well, preacher," he said. "The blackbird tried his gods last night. See him?"

Walkabout nodded. He was immensely weary of Murdoch.

"They've sent us a wind."

"Yes," the other agreed. "A wind to take us to hell! But no food! no water! no land! . . . But I won't be the next to go, preacher." He could only whisper now.

Walkabout looked at him curiously and then he saw something gleaming from under Murdoch's hands. It wasn't the buckle. The buckle was glinting on the after thwart, with a fiber string rove through it now; and that was all that was beside the Kanaka, apart from the coconut shell. The old man hauled himself slowly upright; ran a tongue over his lips.

"Give me that knife, Murdoch!"

And Murdoch laughed, madly. The Kanaka looked across, unperturbed.

"No, no—you crazy bastards!" Murdoch shouted. "It won't be my head that goes first!"

Walkabout laid his arms along the gun'le and gave himself a tentative hoist. But his legs gave way as if they had neither bone nor muscle. He sank back again.

"The Kanaka is a Gilbertese," he reminded Murdoch. "From Tabiteuea."

The significance did not register on Murdoch and the old man said no more. He had known so many wealthy sightseers who never saw or learned anything. It didn't matter much anyway. Murdoch had collapsed again, trembling with the effort he had made.

The sun was half-meridian now and Bu was steering, steering by the shadow cast by the makeshift sail, when Walkabout saw him glance up and stare; and then he stood up and he clapped his hands and pointed; and his grin made a black hole between his gleaming teeth.

"Noria! noria! Te aba!" he shouted, his voice an odd falsetto.

The boat fell away precariously and tumbled into the trough. He lunged back to the tiller but still pointed triumphantly, crouching.

"E koaua! Te aba!"

Walkabout's breath came fast as he strove to rise. He gasped when he made it to his knees. He scanned the horizon ahead and he checked with the Kanaka's pointing finger and he checked again. There was nothing! There was no land! Not a break on the horizon! There was no surf, no reef. He checked again, a trifle desperately now, and then he saw that the Kanaka was pointing into the sky ahead! There was only a little cumulus cloud there, like a ball of cotton wool, drifting slowly across the sky.

He sat back and he stared at Murdoch. Even the native, he supposed, could stand only so much before his reason went. Hallucinations came first. Then—

Murdoch was deadly calm now, and as if he divined the other's thoughts, he nodded.

"Yes," he said. "Plain mad!"

The knife was in his right hand and his body was tensed. The Kanaka was still gazing at the cloud. Walkabout's jaws worked and he couldn't speak, but he sprang first and he never knew how he did it.

He lay on a bed on the veranda of the mission house in Tabiteuea and the world was a warm, bright green even through his closed eyelids. He listened to the chatter of natives voices outside somewhere, and he recalled those last fifty sea-miles; and the boom and smother of surf as they shot the reef, and then the smooth lagoon and the whole native population waiting on the beach in the shade of the splayed coconut palms; and the canoes that had put out to salute them.

And he saw again this Bu, this scavenger of a Kanaka, as they hit the beach. He saw him stagger up to where the women stood, and the shining buckle was in his hand with the string of coconut fiber through it. He saw the girl then, as dusky a beauty as he had ever baptized, run half-way to meet him; and the buckle—the metal buckle that had once held up Murdoch's pants and had later promoted saliva in their mouths—Bu suspended from her neck like a diamond-studded cross.

Walkabout stirred. He thought of the little cumulus cloud that had been alone in the sky and was a mystery no longer. They had failed to read what Nature had written for them—that was all—what Nature, scorned, made visible only to those who would look. There had been a faint, almost imperceptible, green tinge on the bottom of that cloud, and it was the reflection of a lagoon—fifty miles away.

Walkabout opened his eyes and turned to the other bed. Murdoch was propped on an elbow, smoking a cigarette, watching him. He had been shaved, fed, rested; he was a stockbroker again.

"I wondered when you'd wake up, preacher," he said pleasantly. "I've been waiting to tell you something. Know what I'm gonna do?" He examined the end of his cigarette and looked up again. "Well, I like that boy—that bloody scavenger. Bu, or whatever you call him. So I'm going to take him back with me to Sydney. God—I can *use* a man like that!"

Walkabout lay still, scarcely breathing. It was incredible! It was indeed! He was quiet for a long time, listening to the chatter and laughter outside. Then, without opening his eyes, he said very deliberately:

"Murdoch, I was once a 'Frisco pug, as they say. We'll be up and about soon. I'll work you over then. By the time I've finished with you, you won't be able to take anybody to Sydney. And then I'll re-introduce you to one of Nature's gentlemen. Yes, Murdoch," he added, remembering, "and a great lover."

DREAD DILEMMA

Is there a fate worse than death? Aunt Libby thought so . . . and so did the desperate man in her home

CRIMINAL AT LARGE

LARRY HOLDEN

Through the eyes of a child, we can view evil and good in new perspective, sharper focus. Horror somehow seems intensified, and courage ennobled. Which is probably why Larry Holden arranges for us to peer at these violent events from the juvenile point of view. The author claims to have had considerable experience with suspense, being not only a writer, but a Nokomis, Fla., fisherman. The big suspense every day, he tells us, is whether forty cents invested in shrimp bait will bring him an equal return in edible sea life. But that's just niggling, picayune suspense, he admits, compared to the kind in which Aunt Libby's nephew finds himself.

IT WAS raining so hard that my Aunt Libby had to lean over the steering wheel so she could see the road ahead. Ordinarily, we would not have been out on a night like this. But my Uncle Steve was in a Paterson hospital with his appendix, and that's where we were coming from.

You've seen my Uncle Steve in the newspapers. Steve Moynihan. He's the one who showed the police where Howie Russ was hiding in the burned-out barge on the Passaic River, across from our house. Howie Russ is the man who killed his wife with a Stillson wrench. He was hiding in this old barge, and Uncle Steve noticed him two or three times coming on deck for air. Then my uncle got curious and looked at him with binoculars and recognized him.

A whole army of police came after Howie Russ, because he's a big man and dangerous. They were on the river in launches with Uncle Steve and a fleet of cars lined up on the Lyndhurst side. They captured him, all right, but he yelled at my Uncle Steve that he'd get him before he went to the chair.

My Uncle Steve laughed even before the police told him not to worry. People with freckles, like my Uncle Steve, never seem to worry about anything. Even in the hospital with his appendix he laughed and joked with us. My Aunt Libby was worried, though. I could tell by the way she was biting her lip as she drove through the rainstorm.

When we turned down our driveway toward the garage, the water spurted on either side of us, it was that deep. With newspapers held over our heads, we splashed into the house. My aunt was laughing when we burst into the kitchen with the newspapers plastered down on our heads and the rain running from our faces. Our feet made puddles on the blue linoleum. She winked at me as we shook out our coats and hung them on the porch to drip.

"Enough storm for you, boy?" she asked.

I grinned back at her. I was almost grown up. I was twelve. "Not enough thunder," I said.

I kept on grinning. But my aunt was standing with her curly wet head tilted to one side, listening.

"Aaaaah," she said with dreary patience, "It's pooped out again."

I knew what she meant. The sump pump in the cellar. We live so close to the river that whenever it rains hard, the water comes up in the cellar. We have to keep a pump going.

She opened the cellar door and snapped the light switch. The pump was off, all right, and there was an easy ten inches of water down there. In the quiet, we could hear the stealthy whisper of it as it came through the stone foundation.

"Well," she said, "it's fix it or float, I guess."

And she could fix it, too. She could fix anything. Last Spring, when the level-wind on my reel jammed, she fixed it in nothing flat, and still got more trout than Uncle Steve and me.

I pulled on my high rubber boots. Aunt Libby hiked up her dress and pulled on hers, then put on a pair of heavy red rubber gloves, so she wouldn't get electrocuted fooling around the wires on the pump. We went down into the cellar. The water came up to my knees, and even the coal was floating.

The pump squatted in the center of the floor, and she bent over it, tucking her skirt into the tops of her waders. I stood next to her, holding Uncle Steve's tool box.

She reached for a screwdriver, then looked at me and said, "Almost put it over, didn't you, boy? It's time for bath and bed, and this doesn't count as a bath." She splashed water with her hand.

"But I have to hold the tools for you, Aunt Libby. You can't put them down in the water. Somebody's gotta hold them."

"'Got to,'" she corrected. She looked around, then pointed to a small keg beside Uncle Steve's work bench. "Bring that over here and set the tool box on top of it. It'll do pretty well, and I won't have to worry about it taking a bath and going to bed."

You can't win with my Aunt Libby. I set up the keg, kissed her good night and climbed up the cellar stairs as she bent over the pump again.

I closed the cellar door, then tiptoed over to the refrigerator. I opened it slowly so it wouldn't creak. We'd had baked beans for dinner, and there's nothing I like better than a baked bean sandwich. I was just taking the first bite when I heard the footsteps.

The rain was sweeping across the windows like a wire brush, and the wind roared in the trees outside, but the footsteps upstairs were just as plain as if they were inside my ear. I stood stiff with my mouth full of bread and beans. The footsteps came again—cautious, but with weight on them. They were in my room over the kitchen. I knew my room with my eyes closed. The footsteps went around my bed to the closet, to the window, back around the bed and out into the hall. Then they came down the stairs, slow and sneaky.

My heart seemed to swell up and, leaving the refrigerator door open, I dived for the cellar door and clattered down the stairs, breathing hard.

"Forget something?" asked Aunt Libby, raising her eyebrows.

My mouth opened and closed. I felt it open and close. I swallowed the beans. I pointed at the cellar door above us.

"There's a man," I finally managed. "There's a man up there. I heard him!"

She didn't make fun of me. She didn't laugh the way some grown-ups do. She stood and put her pliers back in the tool box.

"We'll take a look," she said calmly. "Give me your hand."

Together, we climbed the cellar stairs. She pushed open the door, and her hand suddenly tightened around mine. For just at that moment, coming through the doorway from the hall was Howie Russ.

Nobody could ever forget Howie Russ. Tall and heavy, with a thick mouth that ran right across his face and faded little blue eyes that kept blinking. He had no shave.

They faced one another, my Aunt Libby and he, both so surprised they didn't move. Then my Aunt Libby gasped, slammed the door and shot the bolt. There was a rush of heavy, clodding feet and the door creaked as he threw his weight against the other side of it and viciously rattled the knob.

"Okay, sister," he said, "stay down there. I'll wait right here for *Mister* Moynihan, and I can wait all the damn night."

Aunt Libby held me tight against her and watched the cellar door. It was only a little ten-cent bolt. We heard his footsteps cross the floor and stop.

Aunt Libby muttered, "Now what's he up to?"

"I think," I whispered, "he's up to the baked beans."

We heard him set something down on the porcelain-top kitchen table, then rattle the knife drawer. When he spoke again, his voice was thick, as if his mouth were full of food.

"In case you're thinking of yelling when he comes home, sister, you can't hear ten feet in this storm. And anyway, I'll be waiting at the door for him!"

He meant Uncle Steve. He was going to kill Uncle Steve, just as he had yelled he would when the police caught him on that barge.

I stammered, "He . . . he escaped from prison, Aunt Libby!"

She said, "I guess so."

"Does . . . does he have a gun?"

She squeezed my arm. "Probably. But he's not after us, Timothy. He's after your Uncle Steve, and we can't let him hurt Uncle Steve, can we? We can't let him find out Uncle Steve's in that Paterson hospital, can we? He might sneak in!"

Her hand was shaking, and her face was strained and white, but there was nothing scared about it.

Then her hands tightened and she closed her eyes the way you do when you don't want to see something. Or think about something.

"Go down, boy," she said suddenly in a voice that sounded all flattened out, "and pull down the switch that turns off the electricity all over the house, the one on the right of the fuse box. Know which one I mean?"

"Yes. It curls over like the handle of a scissors."

"Go ahead, then."

I splashed over to the meter board and pulled down the switch. The lights went out, and the storm seemed to get louder. Upstairs, Howie Russ yelled something, then he understood. "Go ahead, sister," he jeered, "turn 'em off. It's all the better. I'll get him in the dark. He'll never know what hit him."

Aunt Libby didn't answer. I heard her pliers going click-click, and something made a ripping noise. She was working at something.

Maybe it was the dark that made me think of all the police it had taken to capture Howie Russ on that barge; and here we were alone with him. Uncle Steve wasn't coming home from the hospital for five days, and Howie Russ wouldn't wait that long. Sooner or later he was going to come down into the cellar, and that ten-cent bolt wasn't going to hold him back. I felt so scared I must have made a noise, trying to reach through the darkness to the safety of Aunt Libby.

She said soothingly, "Shhhhh . . ."

But I was shaking and wishing Uncle Steve were there. Uncle Steve would know how to take care of Howie Russ.

Aunt Libby said softly, "Turn it on again, Timothy."

I pushed up the handle of the switch. Nothing happened. It stayed dark.

"Now," said Aunt Libby, "get up on the bench. Stand on it. Don't touch anything. This is important! Now do as I say."

I scrambled up on the bench and stood there. I don't know why she made me do this, but if Aunt Libby said it was important, it was important. My heart was going so fast that just breathing was like being sick.

I heard the stairs creak a little as she went up. She pushed back the bolt, and an oblong of yellow light from the kitchen, with her shadow in the middle of it, shot into the cellar as she threw open the door. I heard Howie Russ's chair scrape the floor as he jumped to his feet.

Aunt Libby said, "Stand where you are, Russ. I want to talk to you!"

"Talk to me?" he said heavily. "Talk me out of it? Don't make me laugh, sister!"

He sounded as if he had never laughed in his life.

"My husband won't be home tonight, nor tomorrow night, nor the night after. He's out of town."

"Sure."

"I want you to get out of my house. I'll give you five minutes' start before I call the police."

"*You'll* give *me!* Don't kid yourself, sister. You won't give me nothing. Waaaait a minute. You say the hero's out of town?"

"Yes. It's the truth."

"And you're all alone with the kid. Well, ain't that nice. I just thought of something that'll maybe hurt worse than plain killing. Suppose the hero comes home and finds the kid with his neck twisted? And his wife —" I heard him laugh, then. He could laugh, all right. He said, still laughing, "You're a cute little trick, at that!"

Cute? Why, my Aunt Libby is beautiful, anyone can see that.

"Really worth a man's time. And when your husband finds out— wouldn't that be too bad, now? Wouldn't that be a shame?"

What was he talking about, I wondered.

Aunt Libby said fiercely, "You'll get life for this—you wouldn't dare touch me—"

"Life! I'll get the chair, if I'm caught," he snarled, "Aaaaaa . . ." and he must have lunged at her, because she jumped down a step, slammed the door, and ran down the rest of the way. I heard her splash in the water, just before the door opened again, shooting its oblong of light down into the cellar. He hesitated on the top step, probably looking, but he couldn't see Aunt Libby because she was standing beside the furnace to the left of the stairs.

I saw his foot take the first step. The cuff of his pants was frayed. Why do you remember a thing like that? I remember his frayed cuff and how thick his bare ankle looked. He took another step, then a third and fourth, and stopped . . . waiting, poised to leap back or forward. He still wasn't sure that Aunt Libby might not have a gun or something, I guess. He came down another step, his foot reaching slowly for the tread.

I made out the gun in his hand as he splashed off the stairs into the water. It was a short gun, hardly any barrel at all. He couldn't see me standing stiff on the bench; I was in the dark corner. He splashed another two steps, and my Aunt Libby cried out desperately.

"That's far enough. Come another step and I'll kill you!"

In the oblong of yellow light, I saw him swing around toward the sound of her voice. He still hadn't found her.

"Come on, come on," he sounded mad because she was making him look for us. "You're just making it tougher for yourself, sister. Where are you?"

Aunt Libby said shakily, "Put down your gun, Russ. I'm giving you a chance."

She seemed to be pleading with him, begging him almost!

He turned toward the furnace. He had her spotted now. He stood up straight and I could see his teeth when he grinned and threw up his head.

To my horror, Aunt Libby stepped out from behind the furnace with nothing in her hands to defend herself but a thin three-foot brass curtain rod. Her face looked awful.

She cried hysterically, "I'm warning you, Russ. I'm warning you . . ."

But the rest was lost in the splashing surge he made toward her.

My Aunt Libby screamed, and there was a cracking blue flash from the curtain rod.

She hadn't pushed it at him. She'd just held it in front of herself, and he'd grabbed it. And electrocuted himself. When she moaned and dropped the rod, I saw the wires from the cellar light attached to the other end of it, and when he'd grabbed it with his bare hands, the juice went right into him. And, standing in ten inches of water, it killed him.

Aunt Libby was all right because she had been wearing rubber gloves and waders. And I was all right because Aunt Libby had made me stand on the bench, and I was wearing waders, too. But Howie Russ had been standing in ten inches of water.

The next day, the newspapers all said she was a hero, but I remember how she sat in the kitchen, shaking so hard she couldn't stand, with the tears running down her face, even after the police came.

A corpse had vanished, not to mention a killer. Or was the choir-boy just imagining things?

GEORGES SIMENON

Elusive

"Perhaps the greatest and most truly novelistic novelist in French literature today," is what Andre Gide has said of Georges Sim—who, under the pen name Simenon, *is world famous as the creator of Inspector Maigret. At present living in the United States, he was born in Belgium but at 20 moved to Paris. By the time he was 30 he had written more than 200 popular novels, and while aboard the yacht Ostrogoth was looking for fresh ideas one day when the inspiration for Maigret suddenly smote him. For two years thereafter he wrote a Maigret novel a month, then in 1936 abandoned the detective in order to write "more personal" fiction. In 1940, however, American publishers contracted for 25 Maigret books in English. They were an instantaneous success. Today many American readers rank the inimitable Maigret with Sherlock Holmes, Philo Vance, Michael Shane, Arsene Lupin, Perry Mason and other prime sleuths of mysterydom.*

RAIN WAS FALLING in a cold drizzle and it was still dark. Only at the end of the street, near the barracks, was there a pale light in one window. The rest of the street was asleep. It was a quiet, wide street, bordered by one- and two-story houses almost exactly alike, typical of the suburbs of a sizeable city in the provinces.

The whole section was new, and there was nothing mysterious about it. Nothing sinister or secretive.

Maigret, overcoat collar turned up around his neck, had squeezed himself into the gateway of the public school. He waited, smoking a pipe; and looking at the watch in his hand.

At exactly a quarter-to-six he heard the bell of the parish church behind him. Just as the boy had said, this must be the "first call" to six o'clock mass. With the tolling of the bell still echoing in the damp air, Maigret barely heard the alarm-clock go off

A NEW MAIGRET STORY

Witness

in the house across the street. The sound lasted only a few seconds. The boy's hand must have reached out of a warm, dark bed to grope for the clock and stop the alarm. A few seconds later a light went on in a dormer window. Things were going exactly as the boy had told him. He was the first to get up, making an effort not to awaken the others in the sleeping household. Now he was probably slipping on shirt and socks, dashing water on hands and face, running a comb through his hair. As for shoes, he had said:

"I put them on when I get to the bottom step so as not to wake up my parents."

The same thing happened every day, Winter and Summer alike, during all the period of nearly two years that Justin had served at the six o'clock mass in the hospital. He had said also:

"The hospital clock is always three or four minutes behind that of the church."

Now the inspector knew it for a fact. The previous day his subordinates on the Mobile Squad, to which he had been assigned several months before, had shrugged their shoulders over all these tiresome details of bells and the "first call" and "second call" to mass. Perhaps it was because Maigret had once been a choir-boy himself that he didn't smile. First the church bell at a quarter-to-six, then the alarm clock in Justin's attic room. And finally, a few minutes later the higher, more silvery notes from the hospital chapel.

He was still holding his watch. It took the boy more than four minutes to dress, then the light in his window went out. He must be groping his way down the stairs. He would sit down on the bottom step to put on his shoes, and then take his coat and cap from the bamboo hat-rack at the right of the hall. . . The front door swung open. The boy shut it quietly and looked anxiously up and down the street until he saw the bulky form of the police inspector coming toward him.

"I was afraid you wouldn't be here. . ."

He began to walk quietly, a thin fair-haired little fellow of twelve, sober for his years.

"You want me to do everything the same way as usual, don't you? I always hurry. In Winter when it's dark, I'm scared. A month from now, of course, it will be nearly light at this hour."

He turned into the first street on the right, shorter and even quieter than the one they had just left. Maigret took in a host of details that reminded him of his own childhood. The boy walked at a certain distance from the houses, doubtless because he was afraid someone might rise out of the shadow of a doorway. And when he crossed the circle he kept away from the trees; a man might have been hiding behind them. He was a stout fellow, after all, to have come out every morning for almost two years in all kinds of weather, sometimes in a thick fog or in the total blackness of a moonless night.

"When we're halfway up the Rue Sainte Catherine, you'll hear the second call to mass at the church. . ."

"What time does the first trolley go by?"

"Six o'clock. I've only seen it two or three times, when I was late . . . once my alarm clock didn't go off; another time I fell asleep all over again."

His face looked narrow and pale in the darkness and rain, his eyes were still motionless with sleep; he had a thoughtful expression, reflecting a trace of anxiety.

"I shan't serve at mass any longer. I only came today because you insisted."

They turned left, into the Rue Sainte Catherine which like the other streets in the district had a lamp post every fifth yard. Quite unconsciously the boy walked faster in the dark, intermediary spaces than in the areas of light and safety. A few windows were now lit up. They could hear steps on a cross street, probably those of some worker on his way to an early shift.

"You didn't see anything when you came to the corner?"

This was a delicate question. The Rue Sainte Catherine was perfectly straight and empty. The shadowy spaces between the lamp posts were not large enough to conceal the presence of two men engaged in a quarrel, even a hundred yards away.

"Perhaps I wasn't looking ahead. I remember that I was talking to myself. . . There was something I wanted to ask my mother when I got home and I was going over what I meant to say. . ."

"Which was?"

"I want a bicycle, have wanted it a long time. I've already saved three hundred francs from what I earn at mass. . ."

It seemed to Maigret—or did he merely imagine it?—that the boy shied even farther away from the houses; he stepped off the pavement into the street.

"Here we are. Do you hear? . . . There's the "second call" from the church. . ."

With an utter lack of self-consciousness Maigret tried to enter into the boy's world, the world Justin lived in every morning.

"I must have raised my head all of a sudden. You know the way you somehow feel an obstacle in your path, like when you're running without looking where you're going and you come up against a wall? It was right here. . ."

He pointed to the dividing line on the pavement between a dark space and the light cast by a street lamp, which glittered like gold dust in the drizzling rain.

"First I saw a man stretched out full length. He looked so big I'd have sworn he took up the whole pavement. . ."

This was impossible; the pavement was at least eight feet wide.

"I don't know exactly what I did. I must have stepped back. I didn't run off right away, because I stayed long enough to see the knife sticking into his chest, with a dark horn handle. . . I noticed it particularly because my Uncle Henri has one almost exactly the same and he told me the handle was made from the antlers of a stag . . . I'm sure the man was dead."

"Why?"

"I don't know. He looked like a dead man."

"Were his eyes shut?"

"I didn't notice his eyes. I just had a feeling he was dead. The whole thing flashed in front of me very quickly, as I told you yesterday in your office. The cops made me go over the same thing so many times, you know, that I'm quite mixed up. Especially when I think they don't believe me. . ."

"And the other man?"

"When I looked up, I saw a man standing a little farther on, five yards maybe. Very blue eyes. He stared at me for a second before he started to run. The murderer, of course. . ."

"How do you know?"

"Because he ran off as fast as he could go."

"Which way?"

"Straight ahead, over there. . ."

"You mean toward the barracks?"

"Yes. ."

It was true that Justin had been questioned at least ten times the previous day. Still not a single detail of his testimony varied.

"What did you do then?"

"I began to run too. . . It's hard to explain. . . It must have been the sight of the man hotfooting it away that scared me. Yes, I ran. . ."

"In the opposite direction?"

"Yes."

"You didn't think of calling for help?"

"No, I was too afraid. . . I wheeled half-way around and went as far as the Place du Congrès. . . You see, I took the other street that leads to the hospital, but in a roundabout way."

"Let's keep on walking."

Another chime rang, this time in the higher pitch of the hospital chapel. Fifty yards ahead there was an intersection; on the left the walls, studded with loopholes, of the barracks, and on the right a huge, dimly lit door below the pale face of a clock. It was three minutes to six.

"I'm a minute late. . . Yesterday I managed to be on time in spite of everything because I ran so hard."

The boy banged a heavy knocker attached to the massive oak door. A watchman in bedroom slippers opened up and let Justin in, but he blocked Maigret's path and eyed him suspiciously.

"What's all this?"

"Police. . ."

They went through a passageway, redolent of hospital smells, then past a second door into a large courtyard. Far away they could barely see in the darkness the white caps of the nuns, who were walking toward the chapel.

"Why didn't you say anything yesterday to the watchman?"

"I don't know. . . I was in too much of a hurry."

Justin seemed put out at the idea that the inspector, who might be an unbeliever, was going to enter these hallowed precincts. From his sensitive reaction Maigret understood better what it was that inspired the boy to get up so early every morning.

The chapel was small and warm. Already hospital patients in their blue-gray uniforms were seated in the pews, some with bandages around their heads, slings on their arms or crutches beside them. The nuns herded like a little flock of sheep, in a balcony above, white caps bowing all together in a sort of mystical unison.

They climbed several steps and passed by the altar where the candles were already lit. At the right was the sacristy with its dark woodwork. A tall, gaunt priest was just putting on the last of his vestments, a fine lace surplice. One of the nuns was busy filling the cruets with water and wine. Here it was that Justin had come to a halt the morning before, breathless and with knees knocking together. Here he had cried out:

"A man's just been killed on the Rue Sainte Catherine. . ."

The hands of a small clock fitted into the woodwork stood at exactly six. The bell rang again, sounding fainter than it had from outside. Justin said to the nun as she handed him his surplice:

"This is the police inspector. . ."

Maigret stayed in the sacristy, while the boy took his place ahead of the priest and proceeded, with his cassock swishing about his legs, toward the altar.

THE NUN in the sacristy said:

"A fine little fellow; very devout, and he never tells a lie. Every now and then he misses a mass, and you might expect him to say he was ill. Not at all! He always says that he couldn't bear to get up on account of the cold or because nightmares woke him up in the night and he was still tired."

And, after mass, the chaplain with the clear eyes of a saint in a stained-glass window exclaimed:

"How can you think that the boy made up such a story?"

Now Maigret was acquainted with all that had happened the preceding morning in the hospital chapel. Justin's teeth had been chattering; he was at the end of his rope and in a state of extreme nervous tension. Still the mass couldn't be put off any longer. The nun called the mother superior and meanwhile took Justin's place while he was given first aid in the sacristy. Only ten minutes later the mother superior realized she should call the police. She walked across the chapel and everyone had a feeling that something was up. The desk sergeant at the local police station couldn't make out what she was saying:

"What's that? The mother superior? Superior of what? . . ."

She repeated in low convent-bred tones that a crime had been committed in the Rue Sainte Catherine.

"How do you know?"

Finally the sergeant had sent two men on bicycles to the street in question where they had found nothing at all, neither the murdered nor, of course, the murderer.

Meanwhile, just as if nothing had happened, Justin went to school half-past-eight. There it was that Inspector Besson, a stocky fellow with the look of a prize-fighter about him, had found him an hour later, after a report had come in to the Mobile Squad. Poor little fellow! He had been questioned for two whole hours in a gloomy office smelling of stale pipes and a smoky stove, not as a witness, but as if he were guilty of the crime. Three inspectors, one after the other, Besson, Thiberge and Vallin, had tried to trip him up, to bring out the discrepancies in his story. On top of all this his mother had followed him to the police station. She sat in the waiting-room, sniffling, dabbing at her eyes, and saying over and over again: "We're honest folk that have never been mixed up with the police!"

Maigret, who had worked late the evening before, came to the office not until eleven o'clock.

"What's going on here?" he asked when he saw the boy, dry-eyed and standing on his thin legs.

"This kid is trying to put one over! He claims to have seen a corpse in the street and a murderer who ran away. But a trolley car went by just four minutes later and the motorman says he didn't see a thing. The street is a quiet one and not a soul heard anything out of the ordinary. And when some nun or other called the police a quarter of an hour after the alleged crime, there was nothing on the pavement, not even a drop of blood. . ."

"Come to my office, young man. . ."

Maigret was the first that day to treat Justin with any formality, as if he were a person and not a delinquent child. The inspector asked quietly to hear the story and he listened attentively without taking notes.

"Will you keep on serving at the hospital mass?"

"No, I don't want to go there any more. I'm scared."

This meant giving up something he really cared for. The boy was sincerely devout; he reveled in the poetry of the early mass. Moreover he was paid for every mass, not much to be sure, but enough for him to have saved some money to buy the bicycle of his dreams.

"I'm going to ask you to go just once more. Tomorrow morning. . ."

"I—I'm afraid to go over the same ground."

"I'll go with you. I'll be waiting in front of your house. You've only to do things exactly the same way as usual."

Well, they had covered the boy's entire route, and now at seven o'clock Maigret stood alone at the hospital gate. An icy drizzle still fell from the gray morning sky; sleet stuck to the inspector's shoulders and he sneezed twice. A few passers-by walked along close to the houses with overcoat collars turned up and hands in pockets. Grocers and butchers were raising the iron shutters in front of their shops. The section of town was the most peaceful and commonplace imaginable. It was hard to visualize two drunkards, for instance, quarreling at five minutes to six in the morning in the Rue Sainte Catherine. There was a possibility, of course, that a tramp or common criminal might hold up an early wayfarer for his money and stick a knife into him for good measure. But then there was what came after. . . The boy said that the murderer ran away at his approach, and this was at five minutes to six; but the motorman of the six o'clock trolley claimed to have seen nothing. Of course, he might have been looking absent-mindedly in the opposite direction.

But at five minutes past six two policemen, finishing their rounds, had come by the same way, without noticing anything. And at six or seven minutes past the hour a cavalry captain, who lived only three houses away from the spot Justin had pointed to, passed by, as he did every morning, on his way to the barracks. He too had nothing to report! Finally at six-twenty, the two policemen with bicycles sent out from the local station had arrived on the scene and found no trace of a crime.

Had someone taken the body away by truck or automobile? Maigret wished calmly and unhurriedly to consider every possible hypothesis, but this one turned out to be as false as the rest. A sick woman lived at No. 42 of the Rue Sainte Catherine, and her husband had sat up with her all night. His statement was very positive.

"We hear every noise from outside. I'm particularly alert because my wife, who is in great pain, shudders at the slightest sound. Now that I think of it the trolley woke her up just as she had dropped off to sleep. I can swear that no vehicle except that one went by before seven o'clock in the morning. The first to come was the truck to collect garbage."

"And you didn't hear anything else?"

"There were some running steps."

"Before the trolley went by?"

"Yes, because my wife was asleep. I was just heating some coffee."

"Did it sound like one person running?"

"No, like two. . ."

"And you don't know in which direction?"

"The window-shade was down. It crackles when you raise it, so I didn't look out."

This was the only bit of testimony to support Justin's story. There was a bridge two hundred yards farther on, and the policeman on duty there had seen no car go by. Was it possible that only a few minutes after he had fled the murderer had come back, loaded the victim on his shoulders and carried him off, God knows where, without attracting any attention?

There was contrary testimony, however, that made everyone shrug his shoulders at Justin's tale. The spot to which he had pointed was just opposite No. 61. Inspector Thiberge had gone there the day before and Maigret, who left nothing to chance, now rang the doorbell. The brick house was nearly new; three steps led to a varnished pine door with a shiny copper letter-box attached to it. It was only quarter past seven, but the inspector had been told he could make his call at this early hour. A dried-up hairy-faced old woman looked out at him through a peephole and argued hotly before she let him into a hallway where there was a delicious smell of freshly-made coffee.

"I'll go see if the judge can talk to you. . ."

The house was owned by a retired justice of the peace, who lived in it with this old servant. The old woman said in a disagreeable voice:

"Come in. . . Please scrape the mud off your shoes. This isn't a stable. . ."

The room into which she led Maigret was quite large and the quantity of unexpected objects piled up in it gave it the look of bedroom, study, library and attic, all in one.

"You've come to look for the body?" said a mocking voice. The voice came from near the fireplace where a thin old man was seated deep in an armchair with an afghan over his knees.

"Take your coat off. I thought the police had improved since my time, and learned to mistrust the testimony of children. Young boys and girls are the most treacherous of witnesses, and when I was on the bench. . ."

He wore a heavy dressing-gown, and in spite of the high temperature of the room he had a scarf as bulky as a shawl around his neck.

"So it's across the street from me that the crime is supposed to have been committed, is that it? And you, if I'm not mistaken, are the famous Inspector Maigret, whom the authorities have deigned to send to our city to overhaul the Mobile Squad. . ."

His voice rasped. He was an old, sarcastic codger.

"Well, Inspector, unless you are going to accuse me of being in league with the murderer, or even of being the murderer himself—all of which is quite within your rights—I am sorry to tell you, as I said yesterday to your subordinate, that you are on the wrong track. You've heard, no doubt, that old men need little sleep. Well, beginning at four o'clock in the morning I sit in this armchair, and my mind is quite wide-awake. I could even show you the book in which I was immersed yesterday morning, but since it was one of the Greek philosophers I hardly suppose it would interest you. The fact is that if an incident of the sort related by your over-imaginative boy had actually taken place under my window, I can assure you that I should have had some notion of it. My legs are weak, as I told you, but my hearing is still good. What's more I'm still curious enough by nature to take an interest in everything that goes on in the street. If it would amuse you I could even tell you the hour at which every housewife in the neighborhood goes to do her marketing."

He looked at Maigret with a triumphant smile.

"You are accustomed, then, to hearing young Justin go by your house?" asked the inspector with angelic mildness.

"Of course."

"You both hear and see him?"

"I don't follow you. . ."

"During over half, in fact about two-thirds of the year, it's broad daylight at six o'clock mass the whole year round."

"Yes, I see him go by."

"Since his passing by is a daily event, as regular as the first trolley, you probably pay it particular attention, don't you?"

The judge looked at Maigret with beady, almost treacherous, little eyes. He seemed put out at the idea that Maigret was giving him a lesson.

"Yes, I hear him, if that's what you want me to admit. . ."

"And if he were to miss a day?"

"I might notice it and I might not. One isn't struck *every* Sunday by the absence of the factory whistles."

"What about yesterday?"

Was Maigret's impression correct? It seemed to him that the old judge was frowning, that there was a pouting, sulky, set expression on his face. Old men, after all, are given to sulking like children; they are apt to have the same fits of waywardness.

"Yesterday?"

"Yes, yesterday."

Why should he repeat the question, unless he wanted to gain time.

"I noticed nothing at all."

"Neither his passing by. . ."

"No. . ."

"Nor his not passing by. . ."

"No."

One of the two no's was a lie; Maigret would swear to it. He decided to feel the old man out further.

"You didn't hear running steps below your window?"

"No."

This time the answer was direct and the old man appeared to be sincere.

"You heard no unusual noise?"

"No."

Again the no was not altogether frank, and there was something triumphant about it.

"No trampling about, no thud of a falling body, no death groans?"

"Nothing at all."

"Since you have been on the bench I needn't ask whether you are willing to repeat your statement under oath, should this become necessary—"

"Whenever you like. . ." said the old man with a sort of joyful impatience.

The old servant must have been just outside the room, for she appeared at the threshold at just the right moment to escort the inspector to the front door.

Maigret felt as if he had been tricked. He had the impression that at a certain moment he had been on the point of making an amusing, subtle and quite unexpected discovery, that he had teetered on the verge of success, but had not been able to make it. In his mind's eye he saw the boy, and he saw the old man, and he tried to find a connection between them. He filled his pipe slowly, standing on the edge of the pavement. Then, because he had not had so much as a cup of coffee since he had got up and his wet overcoat was sticking to his shoulders, he hailed a cab and departed for his home.

THE MASS of sheets and blankets rose up like a giant wave, one ponderous arm stuck out, and on the pillow appeared a red face beaded with perspiration. Finally an ill-humored voice grumbled:

"Give me the thermometer. . ."

Madame Maigret, who was sewing near the window, got up with a sigh.

"You took your temperature only half an hour ago." Just the same, she shook the thermometer to bring down the mercury and slipped it in where it would do the most good. He took time for another question:

"Has no one been here?"

"You'd have heard them, since you weren't asleep."

The bed creaked. Maigret's assignment to this provincial city was to last only six months, and his wife had rented a furnished apartment. The light was glaring, there was flowered wallpaper, cheap furniture and a bed that groaned under the weight of the inspector.

"What does the thermometer say?"

"Ninety-nine and a half."

"Last time it was nearly a hundred!"

"This evening it will be closer to a hundred and one. . ."

Maigret was furious. He was always ill-tempered when ill, and just now he looked at his wife murderously, because she insisted on staying in the house and he had an intense desire to smoke a pipe.

"You'd better drink another cup of herb tea."

This was perhaps the tenth cup since noon. The warm water was coming out of him in the form of perspiration, soaking the sheets. He must have caught grippe or a touch of influenza while he was waiting for Justin in the rain, or later while wandering about the flooded streets. At ten o'clock when he had returned to his office at the headquarters of the Mobile Squad, and automatically poked the fire in the stove, he had begun to shiver all over. Most important of all, his pipe did not have its usual appeal, and this was a fatal sign.

"Look here, Besson, if I shouldn't come back this afternoon, you'd better get on with the choir-boy business."

Besson, who always fancied himself a step ahead of the rest, had replied:

"Chief, you don't believe a good spanking would lead to a solution?"

Maigret was too stuffed up with his cold to take such in witticisms.

He went on ponderously with his instructions:

"Draw up a list of everyone that lives on the street; it's a short one, so that won't be much of a job."

"Shall I question the boy again?"

"No. . ."

Ever since these parting words Maigret had been hot and feverish. Drops of perspiration trickled down his face and there was a bad taste in his mouth. He had a horror of illness, because it humiliated him and because Madame Maigret kept strict watch over him to see that he did not smoke his pipe.

But there were moments when it was distinctly pleasant, when he could shut his eyes, forget his age and relive his childhood. He saw floating before his eyes the pale, determined face of Justin. Everything he had done during the morning passed through his memory, not with the precision of everyday reality, nor with the definite outlines of things seen, but rather with the enhanced intensity of things felt and understood by intuition. For instance, he could have given a detailed description of Justin's attic room, which he had never seen at all: the iron bedstead, the alarm-clock on the bedside table, the boy's outstretched arm and the hasty process of his silent dressing, exactly the same, day after day. Exactly the same, that was the point! If a boy serves at mass at the same hour every day for two years, his motions become practically automatic. . . The first bell for mass at a quarter-to-six, the alarm-clock, the higher notes of the chapel bell, the shoes he slipped on at the bottom of the stairs and the door he opened gently into a cold blast of early morning air.

"You know, Madame Maigret, he's never read a detective story in his life. . ."

Although it had started as a joke, by now they had called each other "Maigret" and "Madame Maigret" so long that they had almost forgotten each other's first names.

"And he doesn't read the daily papers. . ."

"You'd be better off asleep. ."

He closed his eyes, after a nostalgic look at his pipe, which he had laid down on the black marble mantelpiece.

"I had a long talk with his mother; she's a good woman, frightened to death of the police. . ."

"Go to sleep!"

He was silent for several minutes and breathed heavily; it seemed almost as if he had dozed off.

"She said the boy had never seen a dead body except in a coffin; it's no sight for children. . ."

"And what does that matter?"

"He told me the corpse was so big that it seemed to block the whole pavement. Well, that's the way a prostrate body would look to a boy. Do you see what I'm driving at?"

"I don't see why you worry about it when Besson's on the job."

"Besson doesn't believe in the dead body."

"Try to get an hour of sleep and then I'll give you another cup of herb tea."

"Don't you think that if I took a few puffs at my pipe. . ."

"Are you quite mad?" She stepped into the kitchen to look at a pot of vegetable soup on the fire.

"I'll wager they really detest each other. . ."

His wife's voice drifted back from the kitchen: "What did you say?"

"The judge and the choir-boy. They've never exchanged a word, but old people, you know, especially when they live alone, can behave like children."

"I don't see the point. . ." She stood in the doorway with a steaming soup-ladle in her hand.

"Listen carefully. . . The judge doesn't dare tell a lie, but he's stalling me off, somehow. The man at No. 42, who was up all night with his ill wife, heard running steps. . ."

He always came back to the same point. His mind, sharpened by the fever, turned it around and around.

"But what became of the body?" objected Madame Maigret, with womanly common sense. "Just don't think about it! Besson knows his job; I've heard you say so yourself."

He sank down among the blankets and tried hard to sleep, but soon he was haunted again by the choir-boy's pale, thin legs.

He went stubbornly back to the beginning, retracing his steps from the public school, across the Place du Congrès.

"I've got it. There's where something doesn't tally. . ."

First of all because the judge had heard nothing. Unless he was lying through and through it was difficult to believe that two men had fought just below his window, only a few yards from where he was sitting, and that one of them had run away toward the barracks, while the choir-boy had dashed off in the opposite direction. . .

"Look here, Madame Maigret. . . What if they had both run in the same direction? . ."

Madame Maigret sighed, picked up her sewing.

"You mean the boy ran after the murderer?"

"No. The murderer ran after the boy."

"Why so?"

"Madame Maigret, I know you'll say no—but it's an absolute necessity. Let me have my pipe and tobacco . . . just a few puffs . . . I have a feeling I'm going to solve it in just a few minutes, if I don't lose my train of thought. . ."

She went to fetch his pipe from the mantel piece, and handed it to him with a sigh of resignation:

"I knew you'd find a good excuse. But, let me tell you this. . . This evening, whether you like it or not, I'm going to make you a mustard plaster. . ."

THERE WAS no telephone in the apartment; they had to go down to the drugstore to reach Besson.

"Shall I tell him to come here?"

"Tell him to bring me, as soon as he can, not a list of all the people who live on the Rue Sainte Catherine, but a list of all the tenants of the houses on the left side, between the judge's house and the Place du Congrès."

"Try to stay under the covers. . ."

As soon as he heard her on the stairs he thrust both legs out of bed, went barefooted after his tobacco pouch, filled his pipe again and then struck an innocent pose between the sheets. He puffed with greedy haste, although his throat was extremely painful. Raindrops were still running down the windowpanes, and he was reminded again of his childhood, of the times when he had grippe and his mother had made him a caramel custard. Madame Maigret came back upstairs, a little out of breath. Her eyes wandered about the room as if she were looking for something out of order, but she did not seem to think of the pipe.

"He'll be here in about an hour."

"I have one more thing to ask you, Madame Maigret. You must get dressed. . ."

She shot him a mistrustful glance.

"You must go to young Justin's house and get his parents to let you bring him here. Be gentle with him. If I send one of the inspectors he'll be frightened, and he's quite stiff enough as it is. Just tell him I want a bit of a chat with him."

"What if his mother wants to come along?"

"Say what you like. But I don't want the mother."

Maigret was left alone, deep down in the bed, hot and perspiring, with a cloud of smoke rising from his pipe, which just stuck out of the bedclothes. He shut his eyes and again he saw the corner of the Rue Sainte Catherine. He was no longer Inspector Maigret, but a boy walking fast every morning on the same street at the same hour and talking to himself to stave up his courage. He was just turning into Sainte Catherine. . .

"Mother, I wish you'd get me a bicycle. . ."

Justin had been rehearsing the words he was going to say to his mother. He must have put it in a more involved way than that; probably he had thought up a fairly subtle approach:

"You know, Mother, if I had a bicycle. . ."

Or else:

"I've already saved up three hundred francs. . . If you lend me the rest, and I pay you back from what I earn at the chapel, then. . ."

Maigret's fever must have gone up, but he no longer had the slightest desire to consult the thermometer. There was no harm in the fever; in fact it seemed to stimulate him. The words he murmured over to himself set up a train of pictures in his mind, and the pictures were clearer and clearer. . . He was a small boy and sick in bed; when his mother bent over him she seemed so big that she would burst her apron. . . The body lay across the pavement; it looked big to a child and a knife with a dark handle was stuck into the chest. A few yards beyond stood a man with blue eyes, who started to run away. . . He ran toward the barracks, while Justin dashed in the opposite direction. . .

"There it is! Justin didn't make the story up. . ."

His fright and panic at the hospital had not been put on. He had not simply imagined the body. And at least one other person had heard the footsteps of a man running. What was it the judge with the unpleasant smile had said:

"You are still taken in by the testimony of children?"

Or at least he had said something very much like it. But the judge was wrong. Children can't invent things, because they need foundation, something to build on. Children may transpose, but they don't invent.

"There it is!" Once more Maigret congratulated himself. He was dripping with perspiration, but he crawled out of bed to fill his pipe for the last time before his wife arrived. Then, while he was up, he opened a closet and took a long swig of rum straight from the bottle. Never mind if his fever rose during the night.

At least this case would be off his chest. And a very neat case it would be, no ordinary affair, but one he had worked out from his bed. This was something Madame Maigret simply couldn't appreciate.

The judge hadn't lied, and yet he must have been trying to play a trick on Justin, whom he detested as if they were two children of the same age. Ah! There were steps on the pavement below, then steps on the stairs and the scuffling of a child's feet. Madame Maigret opened the door, pushing young Justin ahead of her. His heavy wool jacket glistened with drops of rain, and he smelled something like a wet puppy.

Madame Maigret looked around suspiciously. Naturally she would hardly think the same pipeful had lasted throughout her whole absence. Perhaps she had a notion about the rum as well.

"Sit down, Justin," said the inspector, pointing to a chair.

"Madame Maigret, you'd better have a look at the vegetable soup."

When his wife had gone Maigret winked at the boy and said: "Give me the tobacco pouch there on the mantelpiece. And my pipe; it must be in my overcoat pocket. Yes, the one hanging on the door. Thanks, old man. . . Were you worried when my wife came for you?"

"No," was the proud answer.

"Were you annoyed?"

"Well, everyone keeps saying that I made the story up out of whole cloth. . ."

"And you didn't make it up, did you?"

"There was a dead man on the pavement, and another man who. . ."

"Not so fast. . . Sit down."

The boy perched on the edge of a chair; his feet did not reach the floor and his legs swung to and fro.

"What sort of a prank did you ever play on the judge?"

Justin stiffened instinctively.

"The old man that sits behind the window and looks like an owl. . ."

"I've never spoken to him."

"I asked what has happened between you?"

"I can't see him in winter because the curtains are drawn. . ."

"And in summer?"

"I stick out my tongue at him. . ."

"Why?"

"Because he makes fun of me; he laughs to himself when he sees me go by."

"Have you stuck out your tongue at him often?"

"Every time I can see him. . ."

"And what does he do?"

"He laughs out loud in a nasty way. I've always thought it was because I serve at mass and he's an unbeliever."

"So he did tell a lie. . ."

"What did he say?"

"That nothing happened in front of his house yesterday, or else he would have seen it."

The boy looked hard at Maigret, then he lowered his eyes.

"He did lie, didn't he?"

"There was a body lying on the pavement with a knife stuck into the chest. . ."

"Yes, I know that."

"How do you know?"

"I know it because it's the truth," said Maigret gently. "Give me a match. My pipe has gone out."

"You look terribly hot."

"That's nothing. Just grippe."

"You caught it this morning?"

"Quite likely. Sit down."

He listened intently and then called out:

"Madame Maigret! Will you go downstairs? I think I hear Besson coming and I don't want him to come up before I've finished. . . Just keep him company down there. . . Justin will call you. . ."

Then he spoke again to his young friend:

"Sit down. . . It's true also that you both ran away. . ."

"I told you it was true. . ."

"And I'm sure of it. . . Go make sure there's no one at the door and the door is tight shut. . ."

The boy did as he was told, without understanding the reason, but suddenly aware of the importance of his every move and gesture.

"You're a good fellow, Justin. . ."

"Why do you say that?"

"It's true about the corpse, and true about the man that ran away. . ."

The boy raised his head and Maigret saw that his lip was trembling.

"And the judge didn't tell a lie, no judge would dare do that, but he didn't tell the whole truth, either. . ."

The room was redolent of grippe, rum and tobacco. The smell of vegetable soup was wafted under the kitchen door and silvery rain-drops still beat against the black window-panes that shut off the deserted street. Were a man and a child talking together? Or two men? Or two children? Maigret's head was heavy and his eyes bright with fever. There was a sick-room taste to his pipe that reminded him of the odors of the hospital, the chapel, and the sacristy.

"The judge didn't tell the whole truth because he wanted to get you into trouble. . . And you haven't told the whole truth, either. . . Look here, you mustn't cry. There's no reason why the whole world should know what we're talking about. Do you follow me, Justin?"

The boy nodded.

"If what you told me had never happened at all the man at No. 42 wouldn't have heard footsteps running away. . ."

"I didn't make it up. . ."

"Of course not. But if things had happened exactly as you say, the judge couldn't swear that he heard nothing. And if the murderer ran in the direction of the barracks the judge couldn't swear that no one ran by his house. . ."

The boy did not move; he was staring at the tips of his swinging feet.

"When you come down to it the judge was honest, because he didn't dare say that you had gone by his house yesterday morning. But he might have added that you *didn't* go by. That was the truth, because you ran off in the opposite direction. He was honest, too, when he claimed that no one ran along the street below his window. Because the man didn't run that way. . ."

"What do you know about it?"

The boy was stiff as a ramrod, staring at Maigret with the same wide-open eyes with which he must have stared the day before at the murderer.

"There's no getting away from the fact that the man ran in the same direction as you did; that's why the man at No. 42 heard him. The killer knew you had seen him and seen the dead body. You might turn him in to the police, and so *he ran after you. . .*"

"If you tell my mother, I. . ."

"Sh! I have nothing to say to your mother or anyone else. You see, Justin I'm going to talk to you as if you were a grown man. . . A murderer would hardly be so stupid as to let you get away after what you had seen. . ."

"Well, I don't know about that. . ."

"But I know. That's my business. It's not so hard to kill a man, but it's hard to get rid of the body. And this body has made a magnificent disappearance. In other words, the murderer is tough and strong. His life is at stake and if he had a head on his shoulders he wouldn't let you get away. . ."

"I didn't realize. . ."

"It's not so serious, after all, now that the damage has been repaired. Don't worry!"

"You've arrested him?"

His voice trembled with hope.

"He'll be arrested presently. . . . Stay in your chair."

"I won't move. . ."

"First of all, if the whole thing had taken place in front of the judge's house, halfway down the street, you would have seen what was going on from farther away and you would have had time to escape. There's where the murderer made a mistake, in spite of all his cleverness. . ."

"How did you guess it?"

"I didn't guess it. You wouldn't have walked a hundred yards without looking ahead of you. . . So the body must have been closer, much closer, just beyond the beginning of the street. . ."

"Yes, just five houses in. . ."

"When you did see the body you ran. The man ran after you."

"I thought I'd die of fear!"

"He clamped a hand on your shoulder."

"He grabbed me by both shoulders. I thought he was going to choke me. . ."

"He told you to say. . ."

The boy was silently crying.

"If you tell my mother, she'll never

stop scolding me. . . She's always scolding. . ."

"He told you to say the whole thing happened farther up the street. . ."

"Yes."

"In front of the judge's house?"

"I thought of the judge's house myself, because I always stuck out my tongue at him. The man only told me to say at the other end of the street, and that he had run off toward the barracks. . ."

"Well, it was almost a perfect crime. No one believed you, because there was no murderer, no body or any traces of it, and the whole thing seemed impossible."

"And how did you work it out?"

"Oh, I didn't have much to do with the solution. It's a piece of luck that I used to be a choir-boy, and that I had this attack of fever today. . . What did the man promise you?"

"He said that if I didn't do as he said he would follow me wherever I might go, even if the police protected me, and wring my neck like a chicken. . ."

"And what else?"

"He asked me what I'd like to have for a present. . ."

"And you said: 'A bicycle. . .'"

"How do you know?"

"I was a boy once, myself. . ."

"And you wanted a bicycle?"

"Yes, and a lot of other things I never had."

"I didn't want him to be caught. . ."

"On account of the bicycle?"

"I guess that's it. I suppose you'll tell my mother."

"Neither your mother nor another living soul. . . We're friends, aren't we? Just give me my tobacco pouch and don't tell Madame Maigret that I smoked three pipefuls since you came. Older people don't always tell the truth, either, you see. . . Which house was it in front of, Justin?"

"The yellow house, next to the butcher's."

"Go call my wife."

"Where is she?"

"Downstairs. . . She's with Inspector Besson, who was so rough with you."

"Is he going to arrest me?"

"Open the closet."

"There, it's open."

"A pair of trousers is hanging right there. . ."

"What shall I do with them?"

"You'll find a billfold in the left-hand pocket. . ."

"Here it is."

"In the billfold there are some calling cards. . ."

"Shall I bring them to you?"

"Give me just one of them. . . And the fountain pen on the table." And Maigret wrote under his own name:

"Good for one bicycle."

"COME in, Besson."

Madame Maigret looked at the wreath of smoke around the oiled-paper lampshade, and then rushed into the kitchen, where there was the smell of something burning.

Besson sat down on the chair left empty by Justin and shot the boy a look of disdain.

"I have the list you asked for. But I must tell you at the start. . ."

"That it won't be of any use. Never mind. Who lives at No. 14?"

"A man from out of town, a jewel-broker, called Perain. . ."

Maigret's voice came out of the pillows, almost indifferently: "A fence, no doubt. . ."

"What did you say, Chief?"

"A fence. Perhaps the leader of a whole gang. . ."

"I don't understand. . ."

"It doesn't matter. Do me a favor, Besson. Hand me the bottle of rum that's in the closet. Hurry, before Madame Maigret comes back. . . I'll wager my temperature is up. Perain . . . Get a search warrant from the police magistrate. . . No, let me see! At this time of night it would take too long; he's probably playing bridge somewhere. Have you had dinner? I'm waiting for my vegetable soup. There are some blank warrants in my desk. The left-hand drawer. Fill one out. Search the house. You'll find the corpse, I'm sure of that, even if you have to tear down a wall in the cellar. . ."

Poor Besson looked worriedly first at his chief and then at the boy waiting quietly in one corner.

"Hurry, old man. If he catches on that the boy came here you'll find the nest empty and the bird flown. He's tough and clever; you'll see."

Tough and clever he was, too. Just as the Mobile Squad rang his doorbell he was getting away through the courtyard, climbing the side of a wall. It took them all night to lay their hands on him, but in the end they caught him on a roof. Meanwhile other policemen searched the house for hours before they found the corpse, decomposed in a solution of quicklime. The murder was a settling of accounts, apparently. A gangster who was dissatisfied with the way the boss was treating him and who traced him to his hide-out in the small hours of the morning. Perain had knifed him right at the door, never dreaming that at the same instant a choir-boy was coming around the corner.

"What are you saying?" asked Madame Maigret, standing with a hot mustard plaster in her well-groomed hands.

"I tripped him up all the same . . . that judge!"

"What judge?"

It was hard to explain. The judge twisted the whole story, just to get even with the choir-boy and make a little trouble. He had said that he hadn't heard the boy pass. . . But he had omitted to say that he'd heard running steps in the other direction. Yes, old men have their second childhood. They even squabble with children, as if they were children themselves. "Oh, forget the judge."

Maigret was happy in spite of his fever. He had smoked three, no four, pipes on the sly. . . His mouth smacked of tobacco and he could relax and drift off into sleep. . . Tomorrow, because of his grippe, Madame Maigret would make him a caramel custard. . .

Vengeance, fortune and a man's honor rode this bull's deadly charge . . .

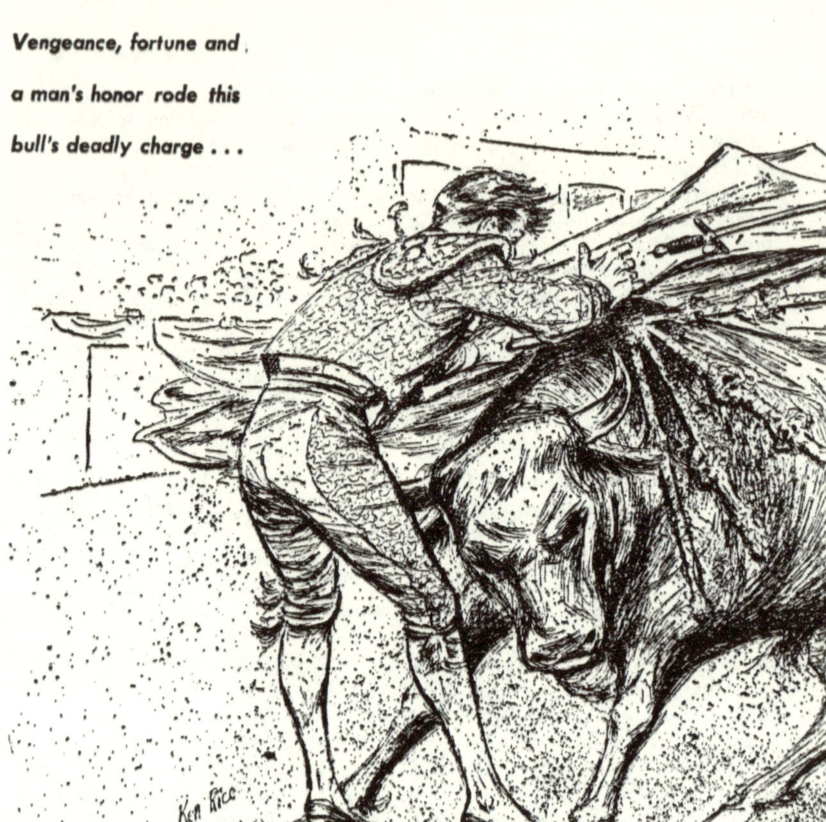

EDUARDO MONTOYA promised to conduct me over the vineyards in the morning. I was weary after my long drive from France, although it hadn't taken many hours to reach the cool hacienda once I'd crossed into Spain. I was on a wine buying mission. But Montoya was an old friend as well as a business associate, and I couldn't help noticing the deep furrows in his lean and aristocratic features, the way he kept gnawing at his lower lip, his restless, shifting movements. "Ed," I called him by the American diminutive, "what's eating you?"

"The devil is in my heart, Stanley," He placed a hand with Latin expressiveness over his left breast.

This was the first time in two years that I'd visited him. His letters to me, exceedingly brief, had mentioned nothing of trouble. Montoya

BLACK DEATH

JOHN KRILL

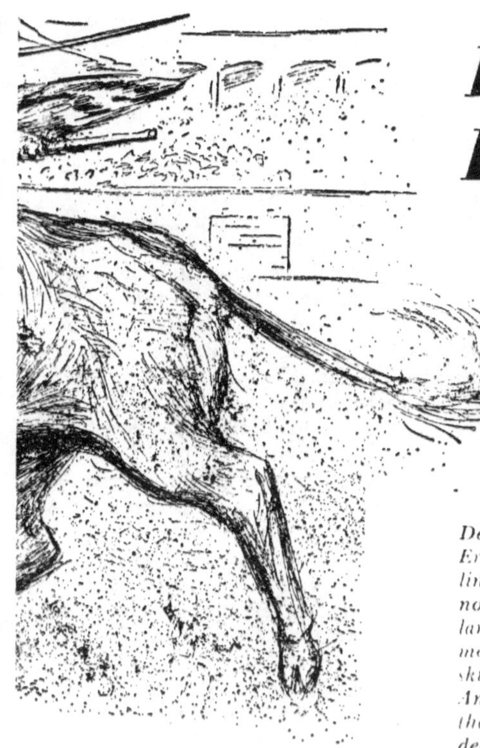

Despite the best efforts of Tom Lea, Ernest Hemingway and Sidney Franklin—not to mention Bizet—Americans north of the border continue singularly unreceptive to the bullfight. To most of us, no danse macabre, *however skillful or beautiful, can justify cruelty. And our sympathies generally lie with the goaded beast. So we can derive deep satisfaction from such a story as this. It relates of life, death and a magnificent gamble—in which the dice, for once, are not loaded against the bull.*

drew in a deep breath and I could see the swift-beating tic just beneath the olive skin at the temple. His brown eyes probed deeply into mine. He was taller than I and much thinner. The thinness was padded by the conservative English tweeds he wore so well.

"Stanley, my good friend," he said in a voice that startled me with its sudden harshness, "we've stood up for each other ever since we met at Yale nearly thirty years ago. But now I am about to do something you would instantly condemn. I'm going to kill a man."

I blinked my eyes in amazement.

"Hell's bells, Ed! You better lay off that green *vino.*"

An angry sweep of his hand shut me up.

Then he told me in bitter words how Felix Lez, a handsome daredevil of a bullfighter, had played with the affections of Marie Rosa Montoya, promising to marry her. Lez then laughed off the promise. Marie Rosa had gone to the bull ring, had thrown herself in the path of a charging bull.

"My daughter lies in peace now these five long months." Montoya's lined face worked with bared sorrow. "But the hours of Felix Lez are numbered. He will meet death in the bull ring even as Marie Rosa did. It is all arranged."

"That's murder, Ed!"

"And my daughter's death was what?"

I couldn't sleep that night. I could hear the breeze stirring the heavily laden olive tree outside my window. I heard something else that made my heart compress with pity and fear for my old friend. His steady pacing over the flagstone walk in the garden below reached me plainly. Marie Rosa had been all that was left after Señora Montoya had died with her second child at its birth.

Perplexed, I tried to figure out whence came the sullen bellowing of an ox. None of these animals were used on the highly mechanized vineyard of over seven hundred acres. Toward morning I fell into an uneasy sleep. My last impressions were the steady pacing of Eduardo's feet and the thundering bellows of the bovine.

Mounted on riding mules, Eduardo and I set out next day to inspect the ripening grapes. "Mules," he explained, "are more careful of where they trod than horses." The grapes with their heady odor stretched in long green rows ahead of us. Red earth separated the lines of green. A snorting and roaring of tractors filled the mild air as tenders began another day of nursing the fine muscat and tokay vines. Eduardo said very little.

"Where is the ox that bellows so loudly at night, Ed?" I asked.

I could see his jaws squeeze tighter together. "That was Black Death you heard, Stan. He and Felix Lez have a meeting next Saturday."

A chill ran up my spine. Was my friend going mad?

I didn't get to see "Black Death." But that did nothing to lessen the oppressing sense of calamity that weighed on me. I could sympathize with him. I had a wife and grown daughters. Probably I'd kill any man who hurt mine. No one knows what he'll do under pressure. Eduardo rode ahead, his proud back bowed, his voice listless as he answered my questions regarding the ripening grapes.

Later I rode into the mountain village that nestled at the foot of the range. Montoya's land ran over the flat plain beneath it. My Spanish was adequate enough to learn from the talk at the cantinas that something untoward was due to happen on the following Saturday. Señor Eduardo Montoya was wagering huge sums of money on his bull against Felix Lez, the finest matador Spain had seen since the glowing days of the great Perez. Rumor had it that the Montoya holdings had been mortgaged to obtain additional betting money. And all the bets had been promptly covered. For Felix Lez was popular, and who in Spain had ever bet on a bull? It was unheard of. I rode back feeling sick.

Saturday came and my host and I went to the ring. The festive crowds filled it like bees fill a hive. Sand gleamed goldenly in the arena. Bright colors, waving flags, the surf-like murmur of thousands of voices, the rasping bellows of hidden fighting bulls, none of these things served to thaw the ice that sheathed my heart. Here was the stage for tragedy. If the bull were killed, Eduardo would be a pauper on the instant. If the bull won, it would mean a crippled, possibly a dead, Felix Lez.

I could sense Montoya's sudden tensing as the lithe, gold-embroidered figure of Felix Lez entered the bull ring to a wild roar of applause. Eduardo smiled grimly as a hoarse bellow thundered sullenly from the heavily barred chutes. I'd heard that bellow before. The warning rumble of Black Death!

Minor stars entered the ring with Lez, and killed their bulls first. They were saving Lez for the climax. Mighty animals drove at puny men in the arena. Always it was the cape they charged, only to receive the steel for their efforts. I began to worry over Black Death's chances. After all, Lez was Spain's greatest matador....

Suddenly I realized what I was thinking. Was I wishing for the bull to kill Lez? If not, was I hoping Lez would kill the bull and cause my friend's final disaster? My mind whirled in a confusion of irrational contradictions. Then at last the slim and incredibly agile Felix Lez was gliding into the ring. The hot sun shone on his heavily pomaded black hair, struck glints of golden flame from his short *casaquilla,* heavily braided and ornamented tight knee-pants faced in gold, tighter silk stockings and light black slippers—all showing off the superb body to perfection. This was Felix Lez.

I glanced at my companion. Never had I seen a face so molded in profound hatred. Thunder came from the right. A huge bull, pale horns sweeping wide from a pure black head, burst past the unbarred gate. He stood pawing the yellow dust, eyes rolling wildly. This was Black Death.

My companion's soft sigh sounded like a prayer. I kept my eyes on the barbaric scene in the arena. Cheers rose from the thousands of blood-thirsty throats urging the confident matador to do his best. Cries of advice pattered down on his ears. Black Death stood uncertainly near the gate refusing to enter farther into the blood-soaked pit. The cheers for Lez turned into hoots and cries of contempt for the laggard bull.

"Who is that rabbit's raiser?" a deep voice bellowed.

"Eduardo Montoya!" a shrill voice answered mockingly.

The cries ran swiftly over the blood-mad multitude. They jibed and jeered Montoya. Risking a glance at him, I saw his face composed and unheedful of the verbal abuse heaped on him. Anger filled my heart. I reached for his hand and gave it a hard squeeze. "Thank you, my friend," he murmured. "Let the fools cry out. They are gazing on their idol for the last time."

Again the icicles began to grow somewhere in my insides. The bull was standing still except for thrusting his massive horned head this way and that as if questing the air for danger. "Throw the mouse out! Throw him into the soup kettle! A sheep has more courage!" came the angry cries from every direction. The bull took a step forward.

Lez began to clown. I'd heard that he himself had accepted most of Montoya's bets, through go-betweens. He tied the red cape to the rear of his trousers, then, back to bull, he ran across the ring. The red cloth waved tauntingly in the breeze that pursued Lez. The big bull ignored the matador.

A rider on a horse heavily padded with protective canvas urged the jaded, fearful nag on with cruel rowels. He headed for the motionless black beast. Jeers filled the air and rubbish flew in the direction of the bull. The frightened horse kept rearing back and whinnying his dread. But the inhuman Spanish bit in its helpless mouth gave it no alternative but that of going on. Black Death ignored it completely. Exasperated howls dinned out.

A banderillero suddenly darted to the huge bull's side and with vicious expertness planted two banderillas in the mighty black shoulders. Black Death leaped forward in a swirl of smoky yellow dust. I could see the shaft of the darts thrusting up from the neck, the little cloth streamers fluttering from them. A mighty roar beat out like the pound of a stormy sea. At last the reluctant bull had been goaded into action.

I don't know much about bulls. I never trusted them after having been chased up a tree by an angry Hereford in my youth. But I sensed that something was wrong with the one in the arena below me. Black Death kept thrusting his head forward and moving with a distressing uncertainty.

The bile grew hot within me as another and another dart was thrust into the magnificent shoulders. Felix Lez stood in an attitude of complete boredom in the center of the ring. His eyes had searched the boxes and had located Eduardo and myself. To my host he raised a hand in a sweep indicating his contempt for Black Death. Old as I am, I felt like leaping into the ring and hanging a good old American uppercut on that olive jaw.

Montoya was always a proud man. I could hear his breath whistle in angrily at the matador's gesture. "Pig," he whispered coldly, "your moments are numbered." I shifted closer to him. Something hard in his pocket dug into my side. I knew what he had there. The feel was unmistakable. It was a revolver.

There was only one conclusion to draw.

If the bull lost, then my friend would shoot Felix Lez and probably himself. What a rotten mess! The lighted match fell from my shaking hand. Eduardo lit his lighter and held it out to me with a hand that betrayed no trembling.

Felix Lez was evidently enjoying the comedy of a bull that was heavily backed with money and which failed to show any pugnacity. Black Death bawled with the pain of the banderillas and wheeled about with hooking horns at the tormentor. A derisive cheer welled from the impatient mob. A side glance at Eduardo revealed him holding a tiny bit of lint plucked from his trouser cuff, in the palm of his hand.

I stared in amazement at his concentration as a fickle breeze moved the bit of fluff this way and that. The fluff floated off in a different direction from its previous movements in the faint breeze.

Montoya sucked in his breath. His eyes shone with a light like that of a feasting tiger's. "Now!" he exclaimed.

Something was happening in the ring. Something startling and to me inexplicable. A long and particularly profane series of jeers faded into a gasp of surprise. Black Death was charging madly across the ring at the idle form of Felix Lez.

I sat frozen. Superb showman that he was—and I had to admire the handsome devil then—Felix Lez scornfully pretended not to see the onrushing beast until the last moment. Like a ripple in a swift stream he moved out of the way. A growing cloud of dust enveloped him.

Black Death wheeled with a surprising agility for a beast so huge. Lez held out the taunting cape. A supercilious smile played on his confident features. A sound like that of a sudden gust of air under great pressure suddenly broke from the crowd. Black Death's horns shot out to reach the man and not the baffling red cape. In the very last limit of time Lez threw himself back. A long and dazzling length of gold braid dangled from his gaudy *casaquilla* where the sharp horn had grazed the lower ribs.

Surprise and fear crowded the matador's features now. His taut face was the dull gray of sour rye dough. Desperately he shook the blood-red cloth in the face of the wheeling bull. A deep silence struck the stands.

The bull had has direction after wheeling. Down on the slender man he hurled himself. The sun gleamed on the sweating black hide and red blood from the imbedded darts shone like brilliant dye against his ebon neck. The widespread horns with their sharp thin tips were leveled at man and cape.

The terrible hypnotic trance in which I was gripped was broken by a shrill chuckle from the man at my side. The chuckle became a burst of near-hysterical laughter. I jolted Eduardo in the side with my fist and he fell silent.

Below me a desperate man held out a cape as a buffer against death. The charging bull was on him again. Again it was the man and not the cape at which the mighty head aimed. Again sheer agility saved the now sweating matador. He suddenly waved his hand for aid as the bull wheeled once more.

That was the undoing of Lez. For that fleeting instant he had taken his eyes from the snorting animal. Assistants scurried into the ring hoping to distract Black Death's attention from the sorely winded and thoroughly frightened matador. But the bull with Satanic wile ignored them and the fluttering cloths.

The sword gleamed with a liquid brightness in Lez's hands now. Hope shone in his eyes that just this once the bull would charge muleta instead of man, permitting Lez to find the vital spot at junction of spine and neck. A great tension stilled all sound in the stands. This was such a fight as none had ever seen.

The bull bore down on the erect figure of Felix Lez. Abandoning the classic style, he drew back his arm. Then like a lightening stroke the sword lashed forward. A sobbing sigh broke from the tense stands. The blade slithered from the bony head as once more the red cloth was ignored. A rag doll went soaring high into the air.

The bull was instantly at the spot where the limp figure landed in a grotesque heap. The ring swarmed with men all trying to haze the crazed animal away from its prostrate and motionless victim. But once again the sweeping span of horns hooked into the gaudy clothes and past them into flesh. Once again the doll sailed high into the air. In a frenzy now, the huge beast began to gore and paw the inert lump of flesh. One of the assistants desperately snatched up the fallen sword and drove it deep into the ribs of Black Death.

The bull stood still for one awful moment. Then it dropped without a sound on the body of Felix Lez.

Next day was Sunday. I accompanied my host to the great cathedral for mass. In my mind I wondered at his serenity. His pockets bulged with the enormous amount of money he had won. I said, "Why are you carrying all that money, Ed?"

He didn't answer. My mind mulled over what he had told me about Lez. Lez was vain and used a specially compounded and heavily perfumed hair pomade. Montoya had secured a quantity by bribing Lez's chemist. Smearing himself liberally with it, my host temporarily blinded the black bull with a painless belladonna derivative. Then he began to beat the chained and helpless beast every day. Unable to see his tormentor, the animal charged by scent as far as the thick chain would permit.

That fatal day the bull with the drugged eyes had hunted down his victim by the scent of the pomade. That was why the cape had been ignored. Black Death couldn't see the fluttering cloth. But he could smell —and he charged directly at the source of the odor.

In church, my host sought out the priest after the services had ended, and placed a huge bundle of money in his surprised hands. "For masses to the repose of the soul of Felix Lez, Father," he whispered.

SUSPENSE STORYETTE

The blind alley, the locked room, the tied hands, the menacing weapon—these are the stocks in trade of your dealers in crime fiction. Is there nothing new under the sun to confront characters in murder stories? Perhaps not. But this author tells a tale with a device which, if not more novel, is at least more realistic. By the standards of Murder, Inc., and certain Kefauver Committee witnesses, that is.

FATAL mistake

Perfectly planned—this killing could not fail. But could the killer?

JOHN BASYE PRICE

In a small California town, late one evening, the two partners in the firm of Morton & Vickers sat face to face in the back of a small panel truck parked in a closed garage. Morton, well satisfied with himself, lounged at his ease and smiled at Vickers. Vickers was not at ease. His hands were tied behind him and his bare feet were immersed in a tub filled with cement.

Vickers, still groggy from the unexpected blow on the head some hours before, stirred weakly. Morton held his flashlight on Vickers, saw that the eyes of the bound man were clearing.

"For God's sake, Morton! What happened? What's come over you?"

"So you are awake again, my dear Vickers," said Morton. "The fact is that I am closing out our partnership." He drew a long envelope from his pocket. "Here you see the profit I shall make from this transaction. No doubt you recognize the fifty thousand entrusted to us by our clients, which you so obligingly drew out of the bank for me."

Vickers licked dry lips. "You're crazy. You can't get away with that kind of money!"

Morton laughed. "No? My dear Vickers, even yet you don't understand the situation. Look at that tub of cement! It is you who will disappear and be blamed for taking the money—while your old heartbroken partner, Jack Morton, remains behind, shocked at the crime. The money, of course, will be in a safe place. And so will you—at the bottom of San Francisco Bay."

"Why bother with the cement?" Vickers gasped. "Why not just kill me and throw me into the bay?"

"Ah, dear Vickers, that would never do. Consider—here we are, two partners, entrusted with a sum of money for investment. One partner disappears and so does the money. Obviously the missing partner is an absconder." Morton paused to light a cigarette. "But suppose the missing partner is found murdered, as you might be if I simply threw you into the water. Even the stupidest cop or most incompetent juryman could fail to catch the implication! So I use the cement. You will sink to the bottom —and never be found—"

"You can't be sure of that," hoarsely urged Vickers. "The stuff may crack. The water may wash it away!"

"Nonsense. That won't happen."

"But I tell you it will!"

"My dear Vickers, I know all about cement. You don't suppose this to be the first time I've used it! This business coup is my own invention. I've been successful with it three times in the last ten years in Chicago, where Lake Michigan is so close at hand. But I thought it best to change my base. So I moved to Indianapolis to find a partner who, though honest, would be less brilliant than I—"

"God, you do hate yourself!" broke in Vickers.

"I simply face facts. I am very clever, but I admit I make mistakes. Indianapolis, for instance, has one drawback. It is not near any large body of water. So I suggested a vacation for both of us—and was delighted when you invited me to visit your brother in California. I had never been west before we arrived. . . . Nice climate, isn't it? I think I shall stay on for a week or so after this—this unpleasantness is over." He smiled. "By the way, how fortunate that your brother should have to be away this week-end. And this truck of his, how nice of him to lend it to us to tour around in . . ."

Morton reached over, tested the cement with a finger. "Not quite hard enough yet."

Vickers desperately tried to move, but the ropes held him helpless.

"In Chicago I always used a boat," said Vickers. But this truck is really more convenient. I can't lift you and the tub of cement together, but all I have to do is lower the tail-board and slide you over into the water."

"Where?" Hope flickered in Vickers' eyes.

"Where no one will see you. It will be too lonely and dark. I have a map here showing a long bridge crossing the lower end of San Francisco Bay. That ought to be a good place."

"For God's sake," said Vickers, "stop yapping! Kill me, then. But get it over with!"

"My dear Vickers. You don't understand what a rare luxury a frank conversation is to a man of my attainments. Only to a person about to die can I reveal them. You know, I always think of everything. That's why I'm not being merciful and killing you now, before heaving you over. You see, there is one chance in ten thousand that the truck might break down or for some reason be stopped by the police. If that should happen, you would still be alive, and

I would say that all this was a practical joke—I had no intention of killing you. The police would not believe me, but a good lawyer could get me off." He poked with his finger again. "I see the cement is getting pretty stiff. By the time we get there it will be solid enough. Time to get started . . ."

Morton turned off the garage lights, opened the doors and climbed into the driver's seat. The truck moved off at a moderate pace as Morton had no wish to be stopped for speeding. After an hour or so of driving, in the moonlight appeared the broad expanse of San Francisco Bay, with the long, low bridge stretching across it. It was very late. Not a car was in sight. Morton turned off the lights, drove out over the water, and stopped the truck with its rear against the rail. First with a weight and a long string he took a sounding to make sure the water was deep enough. Then he lowered the tailboard and started to slide Vickers out.

Vickers had been too dazed to speak, but suddenly he began to laugh. He was still laughing when he went over the rail. Morton heard a loud splash, gazed down at the lapping water and saw no trace of his erstwhile partner. He drove to the other end of the bridge, turned the truck and put on the headlights, drove back to the garage. Nice job, thought Morton. . .

Next morning he rented a car and started out for a drive to enjoy the California sunshine. On a whim, he decided to drive across the bridge for a last look at Vickers' resting-place. The car rounded a hill and the bay stretched before him. He slammed on the brakes. His whole spine sagged. Now he knew why Vickers had laughed!

There were certain differences, it seemed, between Lake Michigan and San Francisco Bay. Last night the bay had been full from brim to brim. But now before Morton stretched mile after mile of dreary mud flat. Morton had dropped Vickers into deep water—at high tide!

With horror Morton saw a police car on the bridge. Several men were lifting the dead Vickers into a van. His brother, Morton knew, alarmed by the victim's absence, would soon enough go to the police and identify the body.

THE MACABRE

Three held stakes in this grim game. But the wanton fates made sport of the winners . . .

PENNY WISE, FATE FOOLISH

MARY ELIZABETH COUNSELMAN

Once voted by readers the most popular short story ever printed in Weird Tales, *where it appeared under the title* Three Marked Pennies, *this closely knit fantasy is among the finest of the kind. Cited by the writer's magazines for excellence of plot, it has been dramatized for stage and radio, and reprinted in England, France, Denmark, Norway and Holland. Its most recent appearance was in the Rinehart collection* The Night Side, *edited by August Derleth.*

EVERY one agreed, after it was over, that the whole thing was the conception of a twisted brain, a game of chess played by a madman.

It was odd that no one doubted the authenticity of the "contest." The public seems never for a moment to have considered it the prank of a practical joker, or even a publicity stunt. Jeff Haverty, editor of the *News,* advanced a theory that the affair was meant to be a clever, if rather elaborate, psychological experiment—which would end in the revealing of the originator's identity and a big laugh for everyone.

Perhaps it was the glamorous manner of announcement that gave the thing such widespread interest. Blankville (as I shall call the Southern town of about 30,000 people in which the affair occurred) awoke one morning to find all its trees, telephone poles, house-sides and store-fronts plastered with a strange sign. There were scores of them, written on yellow copy-paper on an ordinary typewriter. The sign read:

"During this day of March 15th, three pennies will find their way into the pockets of this city. On each penny there will be a well-defined mark. One is a square; one is a circle; and one is a cross. These three pennies will change hands often, as do all coins, and on the seventh day after

this announcement (March 21st) the possessor of each marked penny will receive a gift.

"To the first: $100,000 *in cash.*

"To the second: A trip round the world.

"To the third: Death.

"The answer to this riddle lies in the marks on the three coins: circle, square, and cross. Which of these symbolizes wealth? Which, travel? Which, death?

"Show your marked penny to the editor of the 'News' on March 21st, giving your name and address. He will know nothing of this contest until he reads one of these signs. He is requested to publish the names of the three possessors of the coins March 21st.

"It will do no good to make a coin of your own, as the dates of the true coins will be sent to Editor Haverty."

By midday everyone had read the notice, and the city was buzzing with excitement. Clerks began to examine the contents of cash register drawers. Hands rummaged in pockets and purses. Stores and banks were flooded with customers wanting silver changed to coppers.

Jeff Haverty was the target for a barrage of queries, and his evening edition came out with a lengthy editorial embodying all he knew about the mystery, which was exactly nothing. A note had come that morning with the rest of his mail—a note unsigned, and typewritten on the same yellow paper in a plain stamped envelope with the postmark of that city. It said merely: *"Circle*—1920. *Square*—1909. *Cross*—1928. *Please do not reveal these dates before March 21st."*

Haverty complied with the request, and played up the story for all it was worth.

The first penny was found in the street by a small boy, who promptly took it to his father. His father, in turn, palmed it off hurriedly on his barber, who gave it in change to a patron before he noted the deep cross cut in the coin's surface.

The patron took it to his wife, who immediately paid it to the grocer. "It's too long a chance, honey!" she silenced her mate's protests. "I don't like the idea of that death-threat in the notice . . . and this certainly must be the third penny. What else could that little cross stand for? Crosses over graves, don't you see?"

The other two pennies bobbed up before dusk—one marked with a small perfect square, the other with a neat circle.

The square-marked penny was discovered in a slot-machine by the proprietor of the Busy Bee Café.

He had stared at the coin a long time before passing it in change to an elderly spinster.

"It ain't worth it," he muttered to himself.

The spinster took one look at the marked penny, gave a short mouse-like squeak, and flung it into the gutter as though it were a tarantula.

A Negro workman picked up the penny next morning and clung to it all day, dreaming of Harlem, before he succumbed at last to gnawing fear. And the square-marked penny changed hands once more.

The circle-marked penny was first

noted in a stack of coins by a teller of the Farmer's Trust.

He pocketed it gleefully, but discovered with a twinge of dismay next morning that he had passed it out to someone without noticing it.

"I wanted to keep it!" he sighed. "For better or for worse!"

He glowered at the stacks of someone else's money before him, and wondered furtively how many tellers ever really escaped with stolen goods.

A fruit-seller had received the penny. He eyed it dubiously. "Mebbe you bring-a me those mon, heh?" He showed it to his wife.

"T'row away!" she commanded shrilly. "She iss bad lock!"

Her spouse shrugged and sailed the circle-marked coin across the street. A ragged child pounced on it and ran away to buy a twist of licorice.

Those who came into brief possession of the three coins were fretted by conflicting advice.

"Keep it!" some urged. "Think! It may mean a trip round the world!"

"Give it away!" others admonished. "Maybe it's the third penny—you can't tell. Maybe the symbols don't mean what they seem to, and the square one is the death-penny!"

"No! No!" still others cried. "Hang on to it! It may bring you money. *A hundred thousand dollars!"*

The meaning of the three symbols was on everyone's tongue.

"It's as plain as the nose on my face," one man would declare. "The circle represents the globe—the travel-penny, understand?"

"No, no. The cross means that. 'Cross' the seas, don't you get it? Sort of a pun effect. The circle means money—shape of a coin, see?"

"And the square one——?"

"A grave. A square hole for a coffin, see? Death. It's quite simple."

"You're crazy! The cross one is for death—everybody says so."

"I'd keep it and wait till the other two had got what was due them. Then, if mine turned out to be the wrong one, I'd throw it away!" one man said importantly.

"But he won't pay up till all three pennies are accounted for, I shouldn't think," another answered him.

"He" was how everyone designated the unknown originator of the contest; though there was no more clue to his sex than to his identity.

"He must be rich," some said, "to offer such expensive prizes."

"And crazy!" others exploded, "threatening to kill the third one!"

"But clever," still others admitted, "to think up the whole business. He knows human nature, whoever he is. I'm inclined to agree with Haverty—it's all a sort of psychological experiment. He's trying to see whether desire for travel or greed for money is stronger than fear of death."

"Think he means to pay up?"

"That remains to be seen!"

On the sixth day, Blankville had reached a pitch of excitement amounting almost to hysteria. No one could work for wondering about the outcome of the bizarre test.

It was known that a grocer's delivery boy held the square-marked coin, for he had been boasting of his indifference as to whether or not the square did represent a yawning grave. He exhibited the penny freely, making jokes about what he intended to do with his hundred thousand dollars—but on the morning of the last day he lost his nerve. Seeing a blind beggar woman huddled in her favorite corner between two shops, he passed close to her and dropped the coin into her box of pencils.

It was also known who held the circle-marked penny. A young soda fountain assistant, with the sort of ready smile that customers like to see, had discovered the coin and fished it from the cash drawer, exulting over his good fortune.

"Bud Skinner's got the circle penny," people told one another, wavering between anxiety and gladness. "I hope the kid *does* get that world tour."

Finally it was found who held the cross-marked coin. "Carlton . . . poor devil!" people murmured in subdued tones. "Death would be a godsend to him. Wonder he hasn't shot himself before this."

The man with the cross-marked penny smiled bitterly. "I hope this blasted little symbol means what they all think it means!" he told a friend.

At last the eagerly awaited day came. A crowd formed in the street outside the newspaper office to see the three possessors of the three marked coins show Haverty their pennies and give him their names to publish. For their benefit the editor met the trio on the sidewalk outside the building.

The evening edition ran the three people's photographs, with the name, address, and the mark on each one's penny under each picture. Blankville read . . . and held its breath.

* * * *

On the morning of March 22nd, the old blind beggar woman sat in her accustomed place, musing on the excitement of the previous day, when several people had led her to the newspaper office.

"Let me alone!" she had whimpered. "I ask only enough food to keep from starving, and a place to sleep. Why are you pushing me round like this and yelling at me? Let me go back to my corner!"

Then they had told her something about a marked penny they had found in her alms-box, and other things about a large sum of money and some impending danger that threatened her. She was glad when they led her back to her cranny.

Now as she sat in her accustomed spot, nodding comfortably and humming a little under her breath, a paper fluttered down into her lap. She felt the stiff oblong, knew it was an envelope, and called a bystander.

"Open this for me, will you?" she requested. "Is it a letter?"

The bystander tore open the envelope and frowned. "It's a note," he told her. "Typewritten, and it's not signed. It just says—what the devil? —just says: *'The four corners of the earth are exactly the same.'* And . . . hey! look at this! . . . oh, I'm sorry; I forgot you're . . . it's a steamship ticket for a world tour! Look, didn't you have one of the pennies?"

The blind woman nodded drowsily. "Yes, the one with the square, they said." She sighed faintly. "I had hoped I would get the money, or . . . the other, so I would never have to beg again."

"Well, here's your ticket." The bystander gave it to her uncertainly. "Don't you want it?"

"What good would it be to me?" She seized the ticket in sudden rage, and tore it into bits.

At nearly the same hour, Kenneth Carlton was receiving a fat manila envelope from the postman. He frowned as he squinted at the local postmark over the stamp. His friend Evans stood beside him, pale.

"Open it, open it!" he urged. "Read it—no, don't open it, Ken. I'm scared! After all. . ."

Carlton emitted a macabre chuckle, ripping open the heavy envelope. "It's the best break I've had in years, Jim. I'm glad! Glad, Jim, do you hear? It will be quick, I hope . . . and painless. What's this, I wonder. A treatise on how to blow off the top of your head?" He shook the contents of the letter on to a table, and then, after a moment, he began to laugh . . . mirthlessly . . . hideously.

His friend stared at the little heap of crisp bills, all of a larger denomination than he had ever seen before. "The money! You get the hundred thousand, Ken! I can't believe . . ." He broke off to snatch up a slip of yellow paper among the bills. *"Wealth is the greatest cross a man can bear,"* he read aloud the typewritten words. "It doesn't make sense . . . wealth? Then . . . the cross-mark stood for wealth?"

Carlton's laughter cracked. "He had depth, that bird—whoever he is! Nice irony there, Jim—wealth being a burden instead of the blessing most people consider it. I suppose he's right, at that. But I wonder if he knows the really ironic part of this act of his little play? A hundred thousand dollars to a man with—cancer. Well, Jim, I have a month or less to spend it in . . . one more damnable month to suffer through before it's all over!"

His terrible laughter rose again.

But the strangest part of the whole affair was Bud Skinner's death. Just after the rush hour at midday, he had found a small package, addressed to him, on a back counter in the drug store. Eagerly he tore off the brown paper wrappings, a dozen or so friends crowding about him.

A curiously wrought silver box was what he found. He pressed the catch with trembling fingers and snapped back the lid. An instant later his face took on a queer expression—and he slid noiselessly to the floor.

The ensuing police investigation unearthed nothing at all, except that young Skinner had been poisoned with *crotalin*—snake venom—administered through a pin-prick on his thumb when he pressed the trick catch of the little silver box. This, and the typewritten note in the otherwise empty box: *"Life ends where it began—nowhere,"* were all they found as an explanation of his death.

Nor was anything else ever brought to light about the mysterious contest of the three marked pennies—which are probably still in circulation.

WORLD WITHIN

Dr. Ramsgate got in all right, but the desperate question was—how could he get out?

THOMAS A. COFFEE

This unusual journey through protoplasm differs from earlier trips of the sort reported by science-fictioneers. Instead of a fleck within a fleck within a fleck, we have one fleck conquering others—by virtue of ingenuity, courage and sheer human spirit. Written by a young electronics engineer from Texas now working on (sh! . . . top secret), this story is superb of its kind.

I KNOCKED only once, and Loedstein opened the door himself. Funny thing, I hadn't seen him in months, yet he showed no surprise.

"Good morning. I'm Dr. Ramsgate of the Board of Health. I suppose you remember me?"

"Yes. I've never forgotten your accusations."

"I'm here on rather a nasty mission, Dr. Loedstein. The Board has sent me to expose you, if I can, for what I believe you are—an outright fake! Your sign in front states that you guarantee to reduce any person by as many pounds as he or she wishes, within three days and with no exceptions. That's a broad statement, Loedstein. But I'm a fair man. Admit to me now that you are nothing but a common swindler, in which case I'll quietly hush the whole matter up, and you'll lose nothing but your patients. Or else try to prove to me that your claims are justified. Should you fail, I'll have you jailed under the statutes."

"Dr. Ramsgate, I suppose I should be angry. But I've been through this before, several times. I've sent smarter investigators than you crawling home with their tails between their legs. How much do you weigh?"

"Two hundred and twenty-eight pounds. With dieting, thyroid treatment and constant worry, I'm unable to bring it down. Do you realize I'm more than fifty pounds overweight despite anything medical science can do for me?"

"In that case, you poor man, when I reduce your weight to about 170 pounds, will you be satisfied that I know my business?"

With a shrug I said: "Yes, naturally." And I followed him into his clinic.

The next thing I knew he had me sitting in a peculiar metal chair. Machinery and electronic equipment quite surrounded me. I was all set to start asking questions when he clamped my arms, chest and head to the chair and said:

"The clamps are merely to make sure that patients do not move. There is, however, no pain or physical harm in this treatment. You see, Doctor, you are about to be exposed to thyroid rays. Many men of the medical world have wondered at the possibilities, but haven't the courage to try it. Luckily I am a brave man, Dr. Ramsgate."

I'd heard of the experiments—growth factors subject to electronic inhibition—but the process was supposed to be deadly.

"Why, this is nothing but murder, Loedstein! I walked in here underestimating you. You're completely mad! You know as well as I that you can't get away with this. Not only my office but everyone in the city knows I came here to expose you today. If you murder me simply in order to continue your idiotic swindle, don't you realize the police will come straight to you?"

"Why, of course, dear Ramsgate. They'll be here in a matter of hours, but they won't accuse me of murder. Because I'm not going to murder you, Ramsgate; just get you out of my hair."

I looked him right in the eyes. Yes, he was serious. Panic seized me as he moved about examining various pieces of equipment. Then his hand found a switch on a panel just over my head.

I heard a generator groan, whine, then settle down to a steady singing note. I could see Loedstein turning rheostats and watching various indicators. I felt a scream building up. The scream was just emerging when his hand flashed across my eyes to a push button on the control panel. I heard something. I can't say what. Maybe it was only the click of a relay, or possibly a bomb went off. I can't say. The next thing I knew Loedstein was flicking water in my face.

"You are a nervous man for a doctor, Ramsgate. Nothing hurt but your feelings. You merely passed out from shock. Now please calm yourself while I try to explain what I'm doing.

"You see, I'm giving you the same treatment I give to all my patients, but fifteen times as much of it. Usually one minute of this ray will reduce a person by 20 or 30 pounds. After that one minute I reverse the ray's polarity just long enough to stop the action on the thyroid, and the treatment is finished. In your case, Ramsgate, 15 minutes should bring your weight down, I would guess roughly, to zero pounds. But don't worry, Doctor, you'll be very much alive. You see, this treatment reduces weight by actually reducing size. I'm sorry to inform you, but every part of you will reduce to nothingness. At first you will shrink quickly—until you are about six inches tall. From there on the action gets slower and slower until finally it finishes. It might take years to complete—though in less than an hour you'll be too small to see. Just to make sure you disappear I'm going to swallow you when you are no bigger than a pill. It shouldn't take my stomach acid long to digest so dainty a morsel.

"Let's see, the ray's been on 14 minutes. I'd better get back to the instrument panel. Oh, you can relax for a while. The treatment won't take effect for another full 15 minutes after I cut the switch and—Now! Your treatment is over. I could let you go home but, ah, I'm afraid your wife wouldn't recognize you."

"Let me out of this chair," I screamed. "You're stark mad."

"You'll be able to get out yourself in just a few minutes, Ramsgate."

I couldn't tell if Dr. Loedstein was pretending or not—until the clamps over my arms started getting loose. At first I thought it was pure imagination, then realized with a sinking heart that I was actually shrinking. This maniac had somehow discovered a startling scientific phenomenon and if I didn't do something now, I'd never get another chance. I must somehow escape, and quickly, for according to Loedstein I would soon be too small to do anything at all.

As the clamps continued to loosen, a plan formed. It was possible that the madman didn't realize that I would be free long before I would be small enough to be helpless. I felt well, physically. No ill effects so far. But looking at my hands and legs, I saw that I was already down to the size of a 14-year-old. The clamps felt quite loose. It was now or never.

I watched Loedstein closely. He was rather a small man, perhaps no more than five feet six. Suddenly I slipped loose and lunged at the same time. I landed squarely in the middle of his chest and though I couldn't have weighed over 130 pounds, they were enough to carry him to the floor on his back.

My two small sinewy hands clutched his neck. It took every ounce of my steadily diminishing strength to cling to my hold.

Soon the throbbing at my fingertips died to a soft jerking pulse, then to a slight fluttering, and stillness.

I didn't consider the question of his being dead or alive. I didn't even know if I had intended to kill him or not and lay like one dead myself. Several minutes must have passed before I finally came out of the stupor. My first sane thought told me too much time had been wasted.

I was sitting in the middle of his chest and had been wondering, subconsciously, why his head looked so large, until realization dawned on me.

I was now one foot tall, at most. My wife, Francie: suddenly I thought of her. She would be worried because I hadn't come home yet. I looked at the telephone on a nearby desk. I climbed the rungs of the desk chair and swung over to the phone. Standing on the desk I exerted a tremendous effort and pried the phone off its cradle. I used my whole hand and arm to dial my number. The "zero" almost threw me off the desk when I released the dial spring.

"Hello!" the voice thundered like a loudspeaker.

"Hello, Francie, this is John. Listen, honey—"

"John, what's wrong? Your voice—you sound ghastly."

"Listen, I haven't much time! I'm all right—almost, that is. I'm going to be away for a while. I don't know how long, so don't ask. I've got to figure something out, that's all. I. . . ."

"I can't hear you, John. Can't you speak louder?"

"But I'm yelling now, Fran . . ."

"John, what's wrong! Say something, say something . . ."

No use, I realized then. Though I yelled until my throat hurt, I was too small to be more than a bit of line noise over that telephone.

I rested a few minutes, then climbed back down the phone cable using the silken hairs very much like Tarzan used the limbs of trees. I walked aimlessly over the floor, wondering how people ever could think linoleum was smooth. The mountain in the distance must be Loedstein's body. Just to settle my curiosity and with no plan in mind, I headed for Loedstein at a good brisk pace. The floor was really treacherous, with its pits and crevices.

I wasn't afraid, for some reason. The wonder of the situation, perhaps. My objective for the present was to find out if I had killed Dr. Loedstein. The journey upward through the rough cotton weave of his shirt was a trip I'll never forget. Only determination kept me going, while tiny sharp daggers gouged flesh at every step. Anything can be accomplished however, with enough urge.

Finally I dropped from a low hanging thread, a distance that seemed equivalent to 30 feet, onto the soft spongy neck and climbed up over the chin. Well, at least his whiskers were growing. I stood at the base of a huge one and watched it stretch slowly, but surely; always pulsating at the base where it disappeared into fatty tissue that oozed with oil. It was a nightmare.

Yes, he was definitely alive. The cilia-like fuzz that towered so gigantically overhead was swaying rhythmically, first in one direction, then the other. It was a good sign of breathing. The thought passed through my mind of the great danger I was in. Instinct warned me to seek refuge before this now mammoth thing came to life. But this fear couldn't compare with the one that followed, when in trying to move I found I no longer had legs to move on. During those few minutes of thought a radical physical change had taken place. My whole body, if I still cared to call it that, had softened and combined until I was nothing more than a globule of living protoplasm with slight protuberances where arms and legs used to be. Also I was so small that the fuzz I had been surrounded by was now stupendous vegetation.

Seeing what had happened to my arms and legs, I wondered what my upper extremities now resembled. My head was merely not there. I was looking at my entire body, yet—could it be? I had no eyes, no head, but I saw everything! Well, I considered, the Creator certainly missed no possibility. When I lost the sense normally a property of the eyes, I regained it by a kind of mental projection which is much more versatile, believe me.

I was no longer afraid of the returning consciousness of the body. I was too small and light to be injured by a sudden deep breath or a fast movement on Loedstein's part. But another fear suddenly presented itself. At the moment of physical body change when I had lost limbs, head and eyes, I had also quit breathing air; and the oxygen supply in my new plasmic body seemed to be dwindling fast. This required action! I had slight control of the body by the expansion and contraction method. I wormed myself into a more sheltered area, while thinking about the oxygen problem. After this slight motion I realized how critical the situation was. I was mentally and physically exhausted, and only by perfect relaxation would I live long enough to think out a solution—if there was one.

The only way to obtain oxygen is to absorb it, either directly from the air or indirectly from other sources. I tried by mental control of the new body to absorb oxygen from the surrounding air and I did seem to revive a little: but the poison gases given off by the body I inhabited sickened me to such an extent that I had to discontinue. If only I could separate good air from bad, I would absorb—but wait! In the bloodstream of this body was dissolved pure oxygen, no doubt. The shrinking had slowed greatly now. I managed to wriggle over the edge of one of the numerous bottomless crevices in the skin. I heaved over without a backward glance. The rolling, tumbling fall downward was peculiar. Instead of falling fast and free, I more nearly floated down, gently bouncing from various surfaces on the way. At last I found myself wedged between two jutting, leathery objects that pulsated in and out, and seemed to force me outward instead of in where I wanted to go.

I worked desperately trying to move inward against the outward pressure of gases and molecules of sweat. Each time the structure opened I edged forward and mentally gasped in exhaustion. This could not go on much longer. I was so very weak. But I had hope. I thought I could feel a slight pressure crossing the outgoing one with a force toward the inside, only at a slightly different angle. I changed to follow that pressure. Although weak, it was definitely moving inward.

The farther along I went the easier travel became. I felt dull and vague. I could still feel the never-ending pulsation of the skin structure opening and closing. Long minutes had passed since leaving the outside world. I wondered if Loedstein was moving about now, feeling his throat where my fingers had been, wondering where I was, and if his treatment had served his purpose. I could only hope that, somehow, the intake system of the skin would lead me to oxygen; for I couldn't flex or move a single molecule, only lie pressed between slabs of pulsing structure.

Darkness closed in. I remember wondering about this. A moment before I had been able to see without light. The energy remaining in me must have dropped to such a low point that sight, like thought, was no longer possible. How near dead I was, or how long a time this condition lasted, I shall never know.

As the first inkling of thought returned I knew that all danger had passed. I was comfortable, contented and surrounded by all the elements necessary to life. I was just beginning to see a little and examine my surroundings when I realized the presence of something other than myself. I was still wondering about many things when I heard it, or felt it, whatever it was. In any case a voice within me spoke, not any language, yet in perfectly clear thought. I sensed many individual thoughts. They seemed to come from all directions and penetrate my mind where they all registered at the same time, yet I understood each one separately.

"Found in the externess."

"Heard calls of help. Weak, but still alive. Needed oxygen."

"A very strange one, very complex. Can only understand a few of his thought patterns; must be a top thinker."

"They're coming for him any time now."

The wonder and awe I felt at "hearing" these words was so tremendous, it was almost impossible to accept the truth. Here inside a human body existed an entire organization evidently similar to civilization in the outside world.

I had been picked up, I learned later, by a group of builders who, while working on an outermost cell wall, had heard my mental calls for help. Yes, I could see them now, fast-moving blobs of plasm, darting back and forth to a section of cell wall; tearing out an old part, and inserting a new one, and then repeating the process until a whole section of wall was replaced while I watched. They worked in perfect coordination. Whenever a certain piece of material was needed, out of nowhere a plasmic body appeared carrying just that piece and passing it with no wasted time to the one working at the wall itself.

If I had possessed a mouth it would have been gaping wide open. As I watched them darting through the heavy liquid in which we were all suspended, they seemed like little blobs of oil propelled by some unseen force. I tried the thought of moving. I willed myself to move to the center of the room and I felt the slight friction of the liquid substance against my plasmic body as I moved to the center position. It had been slow motion, but I realized I had willed it slow. I tried again and found I could move at any speed desired. But the faster I moved, the greater the friction, consequently the more heat I felt. This could explain the changes in temperature of the human body. When the body temperature goes above normal, it might simply indicate that the body workers are moving above normal speed, trying to overcome some hazard or destruction.

Having completed the entire cell reconstruction, the workers were filing out through an excretion duct of some kind. I remembered their thoughts referring to something coming after me, and since I preferred to explore on my own time, I decided not to wait to be taken into custody. I fell into place at the end of the line and followed the procession. Their thoughts reflected that they were taking some kind of transportation system to another section of cells needing repair.

I followed along full of expectancy. I seemed to have a greater density than the others. I was almost opaque whereas I could see through some of the workers. We filed through a kind of fibrous substance which seemed to fill the space between cell walls. In most of the cells we passed there were a few plasmic bodies slowly working at some simple task. I could catch a few very simple thought patterns, so simple they were hardly recognizable as thoughts at all. From ahead I received thoughts concerning the next project. From the description it seemed they were to begin repair on a whole section of cells destroyed in a straight even line covering a considerable distance. This I translated as a body cut or scratch.

After traveling through the meshing fibers for a considerable distance, the workers in front of me one by one forced themselves through what appeared to be a solid wall and disappeared. Watching the worker in front bear against the wall and break through left no doubt in mind that I could do the same. So after he was gone I willed a little pressure against the wall. Considerably less force would have sufficed. I went squelching through a heavy mass, through another wall, and into a soft cell on the opposite side.

I felt the puzzling thought wave of a body present, and then an influence of force very uncomfortable to be under. The last thought received from this plasmic body was one of utter surprise that I could move away while he willed to overcome me. I went gently back through the wall and found the transportation system the construction workers had talked about. This I knew must be an artery of the circulatory system. The smaller structures moving, suspended yet controlled, would be red corpuscles.

I was aimlessly carried along, bumping into different things, taking in all the close-up views of medical interest, not considering possible danger. So I was not prepared for defense when out of nowhere a dark object suddenly surrounded me, and closed like a vise, with me inside. I had thought myself pretty indestructible, yet already I felt uncomfortable, sickening as though dissolving into this thing. I analyzed the feeling hurriedly. It was another force, trying to dissolve my structure into his. The only way to fight force is with force. I considered that fact and began a thought to block the force acting on me. It worked. So far, so good. The uncomfortable feeling was gone. The creature acted strangely now. I could feel mental protest at the shield I had erected. Time and time again, the force attacked, until I finally exerted the amount of mental energy I felt was necessary, and the dark curtain fell apart.

Yes, there was danger here; but not for me. For how could one possessing the entire potential of a human body be endangered by the power of a particle.

Under a microscope I might have recognized what tribe of bacteria that fellow belonged to. But seeing him at that size I could only wonder. I passed swiftly onward. The pace was so fast that individual cell walls were almost indiscernible.

Every so often a white corpuscle came close by and I could feel thoughts of considerable power probing into mine, but I gave none in return and they evidently thought me harmless as I was not molested. I soon felt another malicious force. It seemed to come from a quite short distance ahead. I went toward it, and there was a stringy looking specimen, possibly resembling a streptococcus, adhered to the artery wall on one side, facing a mass of whites on the other. I could feel the mingling force of the germ and the white corpuscles. About an even battle, it appeared. I felt like the hero in a story book as I ordered—"Stand back." I addressed the whites with what I considered the small force necessary and they fell back amazed, almost paralyzed. I faced the germ and probed for throught. Yes, here was thought, clear and simple, yet with surprising power. The germ thought, and had a strong will for survival. I knew it was preparing to divide into two parts, and wanted to disappear into secluded tissue somewhere. Well, too bad, it must be done. I decided to try a fair shot of power, just to see the result. I let loose with a tiny bombshell of mental destruction directed to land within the germ.

The germ disintegrated, and also an entire section of artery wall. We were all swept into the surrounding cell walls, which broke down one at a time under the pressure of the blood stream. But this lasted only a few moments. Then as in answer to an alarm, workers from everywhere appeared and closed the break with fibrous material. Within seconds the wall was rebuilt. I decided to be more careful in future.

Soon after this I heard a command that seemed to occupy all space. It was peculiar to understand, yet I had no doubt that it was given especially for my benefit. Translated into spoken words it would have sounded like—"Bring the strange one to me immediately."

The whites gathered around me. They were the same ones who fought the germ plus others who came flocking from all directions.

They surrounded me on all sides, forming a thick wall which nothing could normally break through. Yet they faltered a short distance away, emitting thought of fear and anxiety, reflecting their feeling regarding the task ahead. I mused over the fact that even the innermost flesh and blood felt the same fear that the spirit and body in entirety feel.

These tiny molecules of individual will sent me a thought simultaneously. Though presented as a command, the impulse reaching me bore greater resemblance to pleading.

"You must come with us," they ordered, at the same time almost imperceptibly withdrawing.

"Do not fear so," I answered them. "I will go with you, not because you command me to, but because I am curious about the voice in my mind that came from nowhere."

Traveling in suspension within the blood stream of an artery is a fast process. It was only seconds before we reached a portion of cell wall which, though identical to the rest, must have been the designated place. Here we passed through layer after layer of wall, finally coming to a halt within a cell much larger than the rest I had seen. In the center was a shining body who gave off a greenish-yellow light. He was situated in the heart of a mass of web-like structures that surrounded him on all sides, each thread of web ending in a pool of black oily substance that formed a circle around him.

"I am a controller," he said, motioning me to come to him. "I am sorry the rebuilders did not leave you outside. It would have been better for you to die there and then, for I know ONE will never let so dangerous a thing as you live within this world of ours." The thought received here was of the supreme ruler of the organization. It seemed to be a thought I would describe as one or number one.

"Now you must go to ONE." The whites came forth and we passed through row after row of huge cells packed full of tiny living orbs that seldom moved at all. "What is their duty?" I asked a white.

"You are passing through the edge of a memory section," he replied, and then continued, "here each one of these bodies retain one instant of memory. Their only duty is to keep the pattern of memory sharp and clear, so that their impression may be forwarded to the conscious spirit whenever called for. This is one of the only links with the conscious mind that we have. We run into a lot of trouble here. The memory cells are practically perfect, but often they are unable to get their message through. The reason for this is simple, yet impossible to correct. It so happens there is only one group of nerves in communication with the conscious mind. This is often so filled with the message demanding the memory be brought forward, that there is no channel by which the message can actually be sent. And sometimes the consciousness does not allow enough time for the locator to find the memory cells in demand. You see, memory cells that are not often used become crowded into isolation and are very difficult to locate. Given time to function, this organization would work perfectly.

"We are now at the dwelling place of ONE. We cannot enter, but if *you* go through the wall you will find him inside."

I got the thought and pressed through the wall. It took quite a serious amount of energy to penetrate the massive layer.

At first I thought the cell was empty, and then came a terrific crushing force of power so tremendous that thought ceased, and life itself seemed to ebb away.

Then the force relaxed slightly and I could think again and project my vision to all parts of the place. This, presumably the central room of the entire body, was empty. Except for the peculiar construction of the walls and the thickness of the suspension, it was similar to any of the other cells of the control department. Then a thought exploded within my mind.

"You probably wonder why I did not destroy you when you first entered here instead of letting you regain your senses. Well, you are a stranger to our world. You must possess much knowledge I should like to have. Only once before did an outside power enter this world. He also caused a great deal of trouble, until I crushed him, as I will you very shortly. You agree that I can put an end to you, don't you, stranger? You have felt my power."

"I'm afraid, my overconfident ONE, you missed your only chance. When you caught me off guard and held me under your power, it was possible only because I was not expecting such treatment. Next time you try that, it will be the end of your existence here. You see, when you relaxed your force, I erected a shield against which no power available here can stand a chance. I warn you, the next time will be the last for you."

The answer was exactly as expected. I felt force building against the shield, more and more power behind it. I felt the shield start to collapse in on me. I added power and more power. For a long time the two forces remained quivering between us. I felt the force slowly closing in. This time every particle of power I knew how to use was thrown in, trying to hold that shield in place. Still, the shield backed towards me. This subconscious being, actually only part of a human spirit, was overcoming the whole unit packed into my small plasmic body.

Subconscious — yes, the subconscious, the more powerful agency! I'd have to work fast. I had to draw just a little power from the shield to do what had to be done. When that power was taken away, the shield started accelerating towards me. Quickly I used that tiny bit of power and sent an urgent message to the subconscious part of myself. Power!

Three times I repeated the message, then quickly replaced all remaining force behind the shield. It slowed just slightly, yet still moved in on me. I could feel it closing in, pressing, choking the life from me.

My senses were going. It was hard to think. The dark curtain shrouded me. I felt the spirit shudder, trying to hold on to life. I gave up. Thought ceased altogether . . .

A surge of new strength flowed in. Cessation of thought had released an added force that made the curtain lift a little, and I knew I was not only still alive but stronger than ever. With no further waste of time I sent the entire reserve of fresh energy against the shield. It retreated and closed in on ONE. I didn't stop for a second, but bore down on the shield. It gave slightly, re-composed and then gave again. The second time it kept giving. I heard pitiful pleadings: such thoughts as—"Without me everything will die. You're killing yourself and everyone, not just me . . ."

But I didn't care. All I could see was that I was killing somebody who would gladly have done the same for me.

A few seconds later the controller entered through the wall and I received the thought—"I've lost contact with ONE. What has happened to ONE?"

"ONE is dead," I replied in the same manner. "He tried to kill me, but it is I who still exist." The controller looked distraught, and his thoughts came to me fearfully.

"ONE was the central unit of the whole body! Without him we cannot co-ordinate; therefore in practically no time at all the body will become sick and die and all of us with it."

"Can you think for yourself?" I asked the controller.

"Why, of course, everyone can think for himself, but all thoughts to other points have gone through ONE."

"I see! Well, temporarily at least, this is the way I want things done. Issue an order from——better still I'll issue it myself from this control room. If I think a penetrating thought from this room, isn't it true that the nerve cells here will pick up the thought and carry it to all parts of the body?"

"That's right."

I meditated a moment, then sent the following message to all workers of the body.

"Every portion of this body, take heed. Beginning immediately everyone is to perform his regular duties without contact from me. Send messages directly to each other, or through the controller. Learn to think for yourself. You know the right thing to do, so do it—"

I knew it didn't make much sense to them. Chaos was in order, so I had to work fast.

"Controller," I called, "how do I get to the conscious mind?"

"That you could never do," he replied. "There is a wall of outside etheric power that separates us from the conscious force and matter."

"In that case where could I go to see the outside world and operate the body by command?"

"This I know," he replied, and added—"I have seen it done a few times. From this cell you break through to the transportation directly on the other side. Follow that until you come to a solid mass of message cells. These are much finer than you have seen so far. They are closely woven and carry messages of lights and shadows and color."

He had hardly finished before I was half way there. What a maze of nerves! I passed from cell to cell through the neurons of the optic nerve. Finally they narrowed down into a vortex, and I pushed on harder until at last I looked out upon the world. I could see reflections of the outside world; they thrilled me. Loedstein's spirit of consciousness, I realized, occupied the surrounding cells. This was the center of operations for the conscious world. The I, the *Ego*—the home of the conscious spirit. My would-be executioner. I tried to force through the wall between us. I heaved on the wall with every ounce of force I possessed, yet it held as though by mortal power. I started reason to work and reached the only conclusion possible. Some outside force propped this separating wall. I could only wait. Yes, of course, when the conscious sleeps, the subconscious may take control. So, now being the subconscious I watched and waited.

I watched Loedstein treat his patients—watched the weight rapidly disappear from their bodies. He had actually found a method of dissolving it.

Hours must have passed and finally Loedstein stretched out on a sofa and closed his eyes. I watched closely now. I could feel his memory patterns flowing by, first one and then another—fading and disappearing, each replaced by another, less clear than the last. Finally the spherical mass of Loedstein's conscious spirit drifted slowly to the far wall, merged with it and slowly passed into the cell beyond. Loedstein was asleep.

In the excitement of these happenings I failed to notice that the etheric curtain had disappeared, so I didn't realize until I absently went through the wall that I was in the conscious control room. As soon as I was inside I had the feeling of living again. I felt the physical body in its entirety. It wasn't too bad for an old body. Fairly tired, yes, but not too weak. Yes, I was alive again. I opened the eyes and looked around.

This was the same place, yet it looked different. Colors were different, perspective altered. A strange feeling came to me as I sat up and tried to walk. I could walk, but not smoothly. Each stride was like that of an infant trying to take his first few steps. I remembered there was not much time. With the subconscious organization steadily being destroyed, this body had only hours to live.

I stumbled over to the telephone and dialed my home, got a busy signal and slammed the instrument on the cradle. A fine time to be busy! I sat down on the chair, thinking hard. What could be done now? Was there any conceivable way to bring my own minuscule body back to normal size? A plan suddenly came to me as I dialed again. This time there was a click and a familiar voice said, "Hello?"

"Francie, don't mind the voice. I know it has changed, honey. But I'm John."

"John! Oh, John darling . . ." Then abruptly, "If this is someone playing a joke, it's not funny."

"No joke, Francie. Now, listen. There isn't much time. Rush over to Dr. Loedstein's place, go into the clinic. Break in if you have to, but get in. And remember—when you talk to Loedstein, *you'll be talking to me!* Don't ask questions. Hurry!"

I replaced the phone and ambled around the room. Hurry, Francie. Already this old body was beginning to weaken. Fifteen minutes passed. Then ten more. It would take her forty minutes even if traffic was light. Another five minutes passed. I had to fight to keep in control now. The body was very weak. The conscious spirit of Loedstein realized something was wrong, and I could feel it struggle. His spirit fighting to regain consciousness, regain control.

My own control of his body was almost gone when Francie burst into the room.

"Francie, thank God—now, listen closely. There are only minutes left. Go to the cabinet over there and get a small syringe. That's right. Now look at the clock. Exactly three minutes after I give you the word, insert the syringe into my right arm at the usual place and fill it with blood. Then immediately inject that blood into your own body. I'll be with you then, Francie. Inside you. We won't be able to see each other for some time, but at least I'll be alive and with you. Eventually I'll think of something. Now, wait three minutes, then take the blood—"

"John," I heard her call, but too late. Loedstein had taken control.

The time I allowed was almost too short. The whole body had started disintegrating. Transportation normally used was clogged with waste matter. Many times I had to leave one system for another. Travel was slow, very slow. I saw positively it would be only a few minutes before the entire organization broke down.

I must not be trapped now with liberty and Francie so close.

I reached the spot as near as could be judged and waited, wondering if Loedstein would have come to sufficiently to stop Francie from making the transfusion. More than three minutes had passed. I really began to worry now. Only by chance I happened to notice that just a short distance ahead cellular motion was rapidly increasing. With snap judgement I went full speed for the spot. The only way I could tell I had made it was by the rapid change in temperature. Warmth to coolness and then again to the healthy body warmth of Francie's bloodstream. Safe! Once inside I spent a few seconds killing out the masses of bacteria transferred from Loedstein into Francie. I noticed also the blood type didn't match, but because of the small quantity transferred, no apparent harm was done.

I wasted no time getting to the control room of Francie. Though constructed somewhat differently, a barrier was here too. All I could do was watch, as you might say, over her shoulder.

I looked out at a crucial moment. Loedstein had regained consciousness and apparently his wits also. He had moved about six feet, unnoticed by Francie, and had taken a gun from a small desk.

"You and your husband are very clever, Mrs. Ramsgate, but you won't be around to gloat over it. I know now that I didn't kill him. He has ended my life instead. I can feel my whole insides disorganized!"

I was powerless to help as I watched Loedstein back Francie into the same chair I had once sat in. He was weak; but the gun was strong. As her head came to rest in the specially built chair, I felt her sharp tension under the clamps.

"Goodbye, Mrs. Ramsgate." A relay clicked, the generator groaned, purred—then Loedstein gasped, fell against the instrument panel and slumped to the floor.

His cells could no longer carry on unguided. Chaos had conquered.

"Francie, I guess this is the end. I only wish I could let you know how close to you I am," I thought.

The machine kept running. Soon, very soon, the change should begin. Then what? Would I shrink again?

This waiting, wondering, would it never end? Francie—she was afraid. I could feel it. Every cell of her vibrated. Then I felt it. My cell was getting smaller! I had to get out. I had to save Francie. But how? Already I was too large for the shrinking cell, too large to be carried by the bloodstream. There was only one chance. I took it. The opening from the ear was only a few cells away. Would I make it? I pressed fiercely, smashing walls. Here's the ear. I pushed hard . . . hard . . .

"John, are you all right?—John!"

"Yes, Francie. I seem to be. So it wasn't you shrinking! It was me getting larger. I would have killed you, if I hadn't broken out through your ear. Does it hurt?"

"A little. I don't understand!"

"The last laugh is on Loedstein," I said. "After turning on his ray, he must have reached his final breath and collapsed. And when he fell he must have hit the switch that reverses the polarity of the ray. So, instead of making me smaller still, it reversed the process and I'm full size again. . . . But Francie, why is it if I increased in size back to normal that you didn't start growing also?"

"John, get me out of these clamps. I think I know the answer, don't you? You were so small you drew all the ray's energy. It had to get finished with you before it could register on me . . . something like that."

"Good, Francie! I'm glad you have your wits about you. We'll have plenty of explaining to do to the police, I suppose. But there's nothing to show I killed Loedstein." I kissed her. "You know, darling—if anybody should ask you, you're my number ONE!"

TWO OF A KIND

pardon my TERROR

IRVING BURSTINER

Remarkable, as any editor will tell you, is the way submitted stories often run in trends. One month it will be wife murders or ghost yarns; another, vampire doings. This past few weeks it has been practically nothing but "fiend tales." Of the many which flooded us, this Burstiner story and the Abbott one following it were chosen strictly on merit. But they serve to emphasize the vast differences writers can bring to the same theme. While in both cases the motivation is compelling—abortive and fiend-born fear—actually the two stories are as far apart as the poles in plot, treatment and setting.

Thus does talent ever rejuvenate the arts, perpetually lending fresh faces to the old, essential themes.

THE TALL, angular fellow at the table shivered as wisps of cold fog floated in through the restaurant's open front. He huddled deeper into the brown tweed jacket hanging sacklike over his gaunt frame. His pale gray eyes were fixed on the girl outside. She was a natural blonde, attractive and slim in a tailored mauve suit. The fellow in tweed saw her peel a bill from a thick roll of currency to pay Toni's outside man. He watched her put the roll back into her mauve shoulder bag.

He dropped his check and a dime by the register. The coin rolled off the counter. Grunting with annoyance, the fat proprietor slid from his stool and stooped over to pick it up. The tall man shot a hand over the counter, palmed a pack of cigarettes, and left.

Outside, he approached Toni's boardwalk counter. "One 'burger, without," he wheezed. He drummed bony white fingers on the counter until the hamburger was shoved at him. "Getting chilly, isn't it?" he then mumbled to the girl beside him.

Her face flushed. She set down her

empty glass, tilted her chin higher.

"Come to the Island much?" he asked.

"No."

"By yourself?"

She hesitated. "Yes—I wanted to get away for a while."

He finished his hamburger. "So you came to Coney? Why?"

She shrugged. "I don't know. Probably because I've been reading so much about this place lately."

"Oh." He smiled, but his eyes remained impersonal. "I guess you've been following those boardwalk murders. Strange, but business here is really booming with all that publicity!"

The girl laughed. "That's human nature for you. I guess there's a morbid streak in all of us."

"How about some company today?" he asked casually. "Wouldn't want you to miss anything while you're here."

She laughed. "And you're the official guide, I suppose. Well, lead on, MacDuff."

He shook his head. "No, not MacDuff. The name's Benson—Peter Benson."

"Hello, Peter! Mine's Rosalie."

The banner over the Wax Museum announced in scarlet letters: See our new display—*The Boardwalk Murders*. Benson and the girl followed the crowd inside. In semi-darkness, they shuffled past display after macabre display, pausing momentarily before each one. When they came to the last setting, Rosalie's fingernails dug into Benson's arm.

"Ooooh! The boardwalk murders!" she whispered hoarsely.

Benson's eyes, which had been on her mauve bag, shot to the display. A dim bulb bathed the cubicle in a ghastly green glow that heightened the corpselike effect of the two wax figures it contained.

One figure—tall, faceless, draped in black velvet—stood poised on tiptoes behind a bench. In its claw of a hand it clutched an oversized hypodermic which it was about to plunge into the second mannikin—the figure of a red-haired woman.

Benson looked at the girl. She was staring fixedly at the display, her bosom rising and falling rapidly. Her thin lips, recast in purple by the dim glow, were slightly parted.

Benson's hand crept to her purse. His long, usually nimble fingers were trembling. For a moment they fumbled unsuccessfully with the catch. Then Rosalie sighed, and he withdrew his hand quickly.

"Please take me out of here," she asked huskily. "It's too morbid."

It was after nine when they left the parachute jump. Their merriment had begun to dissipate in the thick fog, and they strolled back along the boardwalk in silence.

"Lovely night for murder," Benson remarked abruptly.

The girl laughed. "Brrr! How your thoughts do wander, Peter!" she jested. "Anyway, it's been swell—at least for me. And for you, too."

"Never had a better time." He hesitated, then added, "Care to look over our big ocean?" He steered her to a bench. He felt slightly chilled.

The lights along the boardwalk were ghostly spheres of yellow-orange suspended in fog. The amusement park noises seemed miles away. Only the crashing surf could be heard.

"No wonder you spoke of murder," the girl said. She set her shoulder-bag down between them. "On a night like this, all sorts of things pass through your mind." She stared moodily out over the ocean. "I wonder if there will be another one tonight."

"A murder?" Benson shrugged. "Could be," he said. "Three Saturday nights in a row—three young women . . ."

"Funny. I could be a fourth, couldn't I?" she whispered.

Benson smiled. "Not with me here." Then—"Say, you don't think I'm the boardwalk killer, do you?"

"Of course not, silly!" She looked pensive. "Still, who knows who the killer is? The only thing anyone knows is that he stabs his victims with some kind of poisoned needle."

"Come now, Rosalie," said Benson, laughing. "I've no designs on you."

"Didn't think you had, Peter."

"Besides," he added, "the three victims had red hair. You're blonde."

"A fine detective you'd make, Peter," she scoffed. "Couldn't that be sheer coincidence?"

"I doubt it," he said. "The murderer is probably someone with a grudge against red-heads. Maybe he was jilted by a girl with red hair—"

She looked disdainfully at him. "Oh, pooh! For all anybody knows the murderer might not even be a man."

"But the papers say . . ."

"Oh, the newspapers! Sensationalism, pure and simple! Don't forget that poison is a woman's weapon."

"But the victims were all women!"

"And just what does that prove?"

He shrugged. "Nothing, I suppose."

It grew even more chilly, and they huddled closer. Rosalie stared broodingly out over the black water. Benson coughed. The girl didn't move. She seemed oblivious to everything but the wild ocean. Humming softly to cover his movements, he succeeded in opening the catch of her purse. Anxiously, his fingers explored the interior until their tips touched the roll of money. Elated, he thrust down his hand to grasp it. He gave a cry of pain. Whipping his hand from the purse, he ogled the bleeding puncture in his palm.

"Peter!" Rosalie's voice had a sharp edge. "What were you doing in my bag?"

Benson's breath came faster. A warm flush drove the chill of the fog from his body. He stood up, gasping for breath. His head spun.

"You! You're the—the . . ." He choked and fell back on the bench. There was a roaring in his ears that grew louder with every moment. As if from a great distance, he thought he heard the girl's hysterical laughter. . . .

The police office was small, poorly lit, and reeked of tobacco. The detective struck another match and sucked at his pipe. He was sympathetic.

"Look, Miss Farris," he told the blonde girl. "I don't want you blaming yourself for what's happened. Benson was a petty thief. We've had him here in the station house a dozen times, mostly for lifting money from girls like yourself. Claimed he couldn't hold a job on account of his heart. He did have a bad heart, you know . . . never was drafted because of it."

The detective's face became grim. He picked up the hatpin on his desk. "Strange . . . a little thing like this, plus some imagination—and poof!"

He dragged at his pipe. "Too bad Benson didn't see the evening papers," he added. "We found the boardwalk killer this morning. He was an interne over at the Island Hospital. Went crazy when this red-headed nurse eloped with one of the doctors."

EVIL is the NIGHT

EDITH SAYLOR ABBOTT

A GIRL named Mabel Travers had been hired to teach the country school at Five Corners. She roomed at the Schell farm, three and one-half miles from the school if you took the lonely willow road.

Today, driving along it on her way home from school in the late October dusk, Mabel was depressed as only a town-reared girl can be when first she experiences the chill and desolation of country Autumn, Nagging her, too, was the realization that she was plain and unglamorous, possibly doomed forever to the lot of country schoolteacher when what she really wanted was a husband, a home and children of her own.

She did have one admirer. Karl, the Schell farm hand, invented excuses to be near her and twice had taken her to the village for the only entertainment available—a movie.

She thought about him now with more annoyance than affection, though she could guess that an offer of marriage would soon be forthcoming. She balanced the security he might provide against the fact that she did not love him or his way of life. She knew little about him other than that he had come to the Schell place in September; he did not drink, minded his own business, was a good worker, and, as such, was respected by the Schells.

Often Karl managed to find the time to walk down the road to meet her. Driving home with his masculine presence on the seat beside her, she was grateful for his attention in spite of herself. Because she was alone in the world, as she supposed him to be, she was sensitive to her surroundings. One evening as they drove along in the gathering shadows she confessed that to her there was something almost evil in the way the dull yellow leaves lay so still on the green slime at the river's edge; in the ominous appearance of a storm in the great, empty sky; in the muted call of the peepers and the katydids.

He smiled quietly.

"You're not used to it, is all. We're afraid of things strange to us."

Driving along the willow road this evening Mabel was thinking that if you loved someone enough you could live anywhere with him, but she knew that her feeling for Karl was not love. On the contrary, he made her nervous with his devotion. His mouth, upturned at the corners, annoyed her with its constant look of imperturbable good humor; his habit of staring at her first amused, then irritated her.

"What are you looking at?" It would pop out almost angrily.

"Your hair," Karl would say. "You've got the prettiest hair I ever saw on a girl." His words were so sincere that she felt ashamed. Her long black curls were often enough a source of comment, but usually in a tone which hinted, "But what a waste! Hair like that on a homely girl with thick ankles!"

Dark was coming swiftly now. Mabel turned on the car lights. She had stayed to correct papers in the hope that by arriving later she would discourage Karl from meeting her as he had been doing. She located music on the car's radio and was comforted.

Her car was not new. When she was sure of her teaching job she had bought a used model and was paying for it out of salary. It had stalled several times of late but she had neglected taking it to the village garage; repairs were expensive. But it had a heater and good tires, and the convenience of the radio was still new and exciting. The music had ended and was being followed by a news broadcast. Mabel started to switch to music again when her attention was caught:

". . . because the trail of the murderer who escaped from the asylum at Bankston has been picked up again, this time in Dan County. He is thought to be hiding somewhere in the vicinity of Five Corners, where he may be working as a farm hand. All farms of the area are being checked. He is nearly six feet tall, lean, strong, with blue eyes and a habit of staring into space. He wears the small, determined smile not unusual in persons of his type. He may be polite and reasonable during long periods of lucidity, but at intervals he is murderously dangerous. He was confined after killing his wife in 1949, but even before that crime he had also killed, for no reason apparent to authorities, a Mrs. Agnes Bedell, wife of a farmer who had employed him. Just before his escape—"

She snapped off the switch and a wave of terror threatened her consciousness. The pieces fit. Karl!

The accelerator felt the urgency

of her foot and the car picked up speed. She must warn the Schells, who seldom listened to the radio until supper was over. It all checked. Karl had come to the Schells in September, the height was right, the stare, the smile, the polite, attentive manner. She wondered if he were still waiting for her somewhere on this willow road. How lonely and dark it was! Not another car had she seen. The river lay at her left. On the whole road there was but one farmhouse, off to the right. It was this house which she was approaching now, just ahead, at the top of a gentle incline. She did not know the people who lived there but the sight of their barn and lit-up windows was welcome.

Half way up the hill her motor faltered, picked up, faltered again and died. Her panic was not too acute with the driveway to the farmhouse so close.

"I'll run for it," she thought, "and telephone the Schells and the garage and stay there until someone comes." She was opening the car door when Karl's voice froze her where she was.

"Having trouble?"

Mabel put her fist to her mouth but did not wholly succeed in stifling the scream. That was a mistake, she knew. You never startled or antagonized an insane person.

"I didn't mean to scare you. Thought maybe you'd be expecting me or had seen me and was stopping to pick me up—"

"I'm sorry. The motor died and my mind was on that and getting up to the house there to phone and I wasn't expecting—I mean—" Her explanation was getting much too long! She began again with what show of welcome she could muster. "I'm glad you're here." Then she had an idea. "Would you please stay with the car while I go and phone the—"

"Wait a minute. I'll take a look. Might be a—"

"Oh no, please!"

"What's the matter? Not afraid, are you?"

"Afraid? Oh no—not at all . . ."

"Well, you needn't be. I tinker with the farm machinery all the time and I won't hurt your car." She could feel his smile in the darkness.

"All right," Mabel agreed. "You look it over and I'll go up to—"

"Stay there," he commanded. "Pull the thing in the dash so I can get the hood up."

She complied, afraid to cross him, and his head disappeared under the hood.

"Try it now," he called.

She did, but when there was a response she took her toe off the starter at once so it would appear that the motor had stalled again.

"That's funny," he said. "I thought sure—well, I guess we're stuck. But we can walk the rest of the way."

In her terror she seized upon the only way of escape.

"Oh, don't give up," she cried. "It's too far to walk and I'm so tired tonight. Please try just once more."

He hesitated, and she thought he was going to refuse. But again he lowered his head beneath the hood and the pocket flash produced its pale stab of light. Mabel tried the starter. It worked. Before Karl could get out of the way she deliberately ran him down.

She felt the wheels bump over him. The car reached the top of the rise, sputtered, died again.

She got out somehow, though her knees were weak. She ran up the drive to the strange farmhouse.

Once on the side porch, where the kitchen light showed warm and friendly, she was even conscious of a thin feeling of pride that she had outwitted Karl single-handed.

Her urgent knocking was answered by a tired-looking man in work clothes. He peered around the door and when she said, "Please let me in. I've got to phone," he stepped aside to make way for her.

"Over there on the wall." He waved toward the telephone.

When Mrs. Schell answered she kept trying to say something to Mabel, who gasped, "Mrs. Schell, keep still and listen to me. Send help. Right away. I have just—listen, do you know who Karl is? I can't hear you . . no, I'm at the neighbor's on the hill . . . Karl suspected what? . . . I can't hear you. Please just listen. Send somebody quick. Get the sheriff . . . you will? . . . oh, hurry. Goodbye." She hung up.

The man was fussing around the stove. He said mildly, "You *are* in a state! Just gettin' me some supper. Here now, the coffee's about ready. I'll give you a cup, strong and hot."

"Thank you," Mabel said.

"Sure," he said, at the stove. "I'm the hired man here," he prattled. "Mr. and Mrs. Boldt had to go over to their daughter in Westbrook. . ."

Unable to bear the heat of the kitchen, Mabel threw off her coat, at the same time letting the scarf slide from her hair. She went over and faced the wavy wall mirror in its cheap frame. She smoothed her hair away from her damp forehead. The dark curls shone, were crisp and springy. One thing about naturally curly hair, it looked good even in disorder. Funny how you thought of such things when. . .

The man turned and was watching her with a smile. He stared at her hair and stated flatly, "You've got black, curly hair." Mabel hardly heard. She put the backs of both hands under her long bob and flung it out away from her neck to feel the coolness.

Still looking absently in the mirror she had time to see the flash of the knife as it descended to its mark and before eternal darkness engulfed her she heard, diminishing in tone, a man's voice, repeating, "Black, curly hair like my cheating wife had; the farm woman, too. I cried when I killed her because she had black hair like my wife's, and now you—you—"

HIGH DRAMA

In each issue, the magazine Suspense *features one of the distinguished short plays which have made broadcasting history as part of the CBS radio-television program series* Suspense. Maiden Beware, *published below, was originally performed over the CBS network in July, 1944, under the title* The Black Shawl, *starring Dame May Whitty and Maureen O'Sullivan.*

Numbering its audience in the millions, the CBS Suspense *series has brought to perfection a new type of high-tension presentation, in harmony with modern tastes, and featuring advanced concepts of entertainment. It ranks today as one of the finest dramatic programs on the air.*

Maiden Beware

RICHARD LEWIS

THE *scene is a county fair in North England, toward evening. Gay, noisy crowds throng the exhibits, jostling each other good-naturedly.* Susan, *young and bright-eyed, stands, back to the flower booth, whistling* Drink to Me Only With Thine Eyes. *A group of acquaintances strolls by.*

GIRL: Susan! Not waiting for Rob again, are you?

SUSAN: When have you seen me that I haven't been?

GIRL: And him the solicitor for the watch factory. They ought to teach him to tell time. (*All laugh*)

MAN: How about a dance, Sue?

SUSAN: Thanks, George, but I'd rather wait. He'll be along. (*They move off, laughing. Susan resumes whistling. An old woman in black, who has been covertly watching the girl suddenly speaks.*)

MRS. M: Hello, there.

SUSAN: (*Stops whistling abruptly*) Oh, hello. Do I know you?

MRS. M: No. But I've been watching you, and I wondered whom you were waiting for.

SUSAN: Just a friend.

MRS. M: I see. I don't wish to seem inquisitive, please don't misunderstand. It's only that your face struck me as being unusually bright and alive—as well as uncommonly pretty. You see, I have an eye for faces. My son was a sculptor. He worked almost entirely with heads, and my job was choosing them. It's all very foolish, I'll admit, more so since he . . . departed some time ago.

SUSAN: (*Sympathetically*) Oh, I'm sorry.

MRS. M: But that isn't precisely why I was watching you. You see, it wasn't as a model I was thinking of you. (*Quickly*) I know nothing about you, no more than you do of me, but . . . by the way, what is your name?

SUSAN: Susan Appleby.

MRS. M: Mine is Elizabeth Masters. I live just the other side of town. Let me come to the point, Susan. I admire your looks, and I like the way you act and speak. I'm not a young woman, and I'm lonely. (*Sad*) I have been ever since I lost my son. I need a companion, someone who can stay with me and help me, too. And you resemble closely my very first companion, my best remembered one.

SUSAN: But . . .

MRS. M: I'll pay you well, thirty pounds a month. (*Laughs*) Your chief occupation will be to brew me some tea and talk to me. Are you interested?

SUSAN: That's funny! I've been seeking just that sort of position. But . . .

MRS. M: Splendid! You need look no longer.

SUSAN: But you know nothing about me!

MRS. M: I know that I like you, and I want you to accept my offer. I will return here at this same time tomorrow. If you want the position, please be here . . . and believe me, I hope you are here. Good night, Susan.

SUSAN: (*Still startled*) Good night. (*Whistles* Drink to Me Only. . .)

ROB: (*Coming up behind her, he joins in whistling. They both stop*) What does she mean, please be here? I thought you were expecting me? What do you think you're doing, making dates with strange women? And—she really looks strange!

SUSAN: Mrs. Masters? Oh, no. She's nice. And Rob, she offered me a position—as a companion, just what I wanted . . . and at thirty pounds a month, darling.

ROB: No small sum, that.

SUSAN: I'm thinking seriously of it, Rob. I'm going to take it.

ROB: What do you know about the old hen?

SUSAN: Why, nothing yet.

ROB: Did you look at the way she dressed, Sue? Black from shoes to shawl . . . why, you'd hardly know she had a face under that black shawl.

SUSAN: She seemed charming.

ROB: And well she might be. But I'm not so bad myself. And I want you for a companion, too. Let's push the wedding date ahead, darling. Make it any time you will.

SUSAN: We've gone through that so many times, and you know it can't be done. But, the way you're coming along, and thirty pounds a month additional. . .why, we'll have all we need in no time.

ROB: You're an awfully stubborn fellow, darling.

SUSAN: You know I'm right.

ROB: How many evenings off will she allow you?

SUSAN: We didn't get that far.

ROB: Where's her place, then?

Susan: Why . . . that's strange, isn't it? She left so quickly I never had a chance to ask. (*Pause*)

Rob: Call it off, Sue.

Susan: Why, Rob?

Rob: I don't like it. You nothing about her. Not even where she lives.

Susan: I told you, I hardly spoke to her. Tomorrow I'll know everything.

Rob: (*Reluctantly*) All right, my darling, you win . . . but let me hear from you as soon as you're set. (*He kisses her*)

Susan: Of course. Everything will be fine, dear.

The following night, Susan waits as instructed. Mrs. Masters picks the girl up in her car. The trip is short, not over two miles from town, but with so many twistings and turnings that Susan is completely confused. Finally the car stops before an old, dark house surrounded by dank hedge. Susan, nervous, is reassured when she sees her cheerful, comfortable room. She freshens up and goes downstairs.

Mrs. M: I'm in the parlor, over here, Miss Appleby. Won't you join me in a cup of tea?

Susan: Thank you, Mrs. Masters. I *love* my room.

Mrs. M: Good. Sit down over there, opposite me, won't you?

Susan: I certainly will. The fire's as inviting as the tea.

Mrs. M: Keep one burning whenever I'm home. I get cold so easily—that's why I always wear this shawl about me. (*Pouring tea*) Now, Susan, tell me about yourself . . . everything, all you've done, all you see in the future for yourself.

Susan: There's little to tell. I've always lived here in town, and expect I always shall.

Mrs. M: After you're married, you mean. I presume you've a young man.

Susan: Oh, yes.

Mrs. M: (*Reminiscent*) It *is* the only thing that matters, isn't it, having someone to care for? I know. Before my son left me, I desired nothing. The scope of his talent was the world we lived in—and very beautiful. I suppose love is like talent in that respect. It, too, creates a smaller world within the large one we inhabit.

Susan: (*Interested*) Talent? What kind?

Mrs. M: Everyone saw in his work the promise of a truly great sculptor. The promise never bore fruit . . . because he hadn't enough time. I lost him far too early. . . .

Susan: How old was he?

Mrs. M: (*With great emotion*) I lost him before his thirtieth birthday.

Susan: That's so terrible . . . such a waste. . . .

Mrs. M: That's it! You realize it, too, the waste. Genius cast away . . . killed before it reached full expression. That no one can forget . . . (*Almost sobbing*)

Susan: Please, Mrs. Masters, we have no control over such matters. They're God's will.

Mrs. M: Of course. Thank you. You're very sweet. I wish you more success in the world of *your* love. Remember my son . . . life can be so short. Enjoy it while you may!

Susan goes to her room, sleeps well, rises later than she intended. She dresses quickly and runs downstairs. She finds a note on the kitchen table telling her that Mrs. Masters has gone shopping. Susan makes herself breakfast, then looks around for a telephone in order to call Rob. She can find none. She decides to go out for a bit of fresh air. She tries the front door. It is locked—from the outside. Surprised, she returns to the kitchen, notices for the first time that all the windows are barred. She rushes to the back door, puts her hand on the knob . . . But at that moment the heavy lock turns and the door opens inward.

SUSAN: Oh!

MRS. M: (*Calm, cold*) Susan . . . Good morning. Did you have a good night's rest?

SUSAN: (*Upset*) Well, yes, thank you.

MRS. M: Fine . . . But you're trembling! Is there a chill in the house? You really should stay away from the doors.

SUSAN: Why? I wanted a breath of air. The front door is locked. . .

MRS. M: Is it? I must have done it automatically. I've lived alone so long. . . It's only natural for a lone person to lock all doors when they go out.

SUSAN: (*Still upset*) Why are the windows barred?

MRS. M: Oh, that! It goes back to the time my son did his work here. We had so much of it lying carelessly around the house—so much of value. Anyone might have easily climbed through the windows.

SUSAN: Of course! How silly of me. For a moment, though, I felt like a prisoner behind bars. (*Laughs*)

MRS. M: (*Laughs also, coldly*) Now you're smiling again. That's fine. My son always liked to see a smile on a woman's face. Without one, he always said, they reminded him of death. (*Pause*) Yes. (*Pause*)

In her room later, Susan writes a letter to Rob.

SUSAN: (*Reading aloud*) Please come to see me, right now, Rob, if you can. Everything's all right, don't worry about me, but come to me. It's unbelievable, but I must tell you I still don't know the address here and I can't tell you how to find the place. But someone must know Mrs. Masters and can tell you where she lives. I want to send this off to you now, so I'll close. I can't tell you, darling, how great is my need to see you, and my love for you. . .

She seals letter, descends stairs and finds Mrs. Masters in the kitchen.

MRS. M: (*Surprised*) Why, yes, Susan, what is it?

SUSAN: Where do you send outgoing mail?

MRS. M: Oh, just let me have whatever you want mailed and I'll drop it in the box when I go shopping tomorrow.

SUSAN: Well, I don't want to bother you. I'll take it down myself.

MRS. M: No bother at all. There's no place around here to mail a letter, but I pass the box nearly every day.

SUSAN: But, I'd rather. . .

MRS. M: It's settled. . .let me have

it. It will be sent early tomorrow.

SUSAN: Of course, here you are.

MRS. M: Good. And, Susan, I dropped my shawl—would you mind?

SUSAN: Not at all.

MRS. M: Exquisite, isn't it? Will you join me in a cup of tea?

SUSAN: No, thank you. (*Embarrassed*) Mrs. Masters, this morning I said I was silly for feeling like a prisoner here. But the feeling persists.

MRS. M: Why, what have I done, child, to create that impression?

SUSAN: I'm not trying to answer that question—it's something I just feel. The question I'd really like answered is, what do you want with me? (*Sound of crash is heard coming from upstairs*)

MRS. M: (*Jumping up so hastily that she overturns tea things*) Wait here. I'll be back shortly. Wait right here, understand? (*Goes off*)

SUSAN: (*Running after her*) No I won't stay here. I'm frightened. If you're going upstairs, I'm going with you. (*Mrs. Masters is already out of sight. Susan climbs to the top of stairs, stops, hears the old lady's voice*)

MRS. M: (*Behind closed door*) No, don't worry about the bust, dear. It hasn't been broken. (*Sound of man whimpering*) There, there, don't cry, dear. . .

SUSAN: (*Screams. Flings open door*) Who. . .that man!

MRS. M: (*Furious*) Susan! I told you to stay downstairs. (*Suddenly calm*) Oh, what's the difference? You had to know sooner or later. Miss Appleby, this is John Masters, my son.

JOHN: (*Gibbers and grunts*)

That evening, there are three at dinner. Susan cannot bear to look at John's twisted face, his dull, glazed eyes. He whimpers, grunts, is unable to speak a single intelligible word. And watching Mrs. Masters, with her black shawl draped around her, Susan begins to feel that the old woman is as mad as her son. By now she is keenly aware of her danger.

Later the same night, in her own room, she silently packs her bag. She waits till shortly after midnight, then opens her door and looks out. All is dark. She starts down the stairs, tiptoes toward the front door.

MRS. M: Susan? (*Switches on light*)

SUSAN: (*Suppresses scream*) Oh!

MRS. M: (*Evenly*) Susan, where do you think you're going? You couldn't possibly find your way about, once outside the house. You'd get hopelessly lost. (*To John, who has just appeared beside her*) Wouldn't she, son? (*He grunts*)

SUSAN: (*Crying*) Stop it!

MRS. M: All right. John, leave us now. John, did you hear me? (*He grunts, shuffles off*)

SUSAN: (*Frightened*) Mrs. Masters, you've no right to keep me here if I don't wish to stay. When I accepted the position, I was of the opinion that you lived alone. Since the conditions are different, I wish now to leave.

MRS. M: (*Pleading*) I don't blame you. Please, Susan . . . believe me, I don't blame you a bit. But think of me, just for a single moment. Why do you think I asked you here? Do you believe it's so easy for me, chained to this lost thing, unable to converse with anyone day or night? I needed someone . . . I need someone now. . . .

SUSAN: You told me he was dead.

MRS. M: I never told you that—only that he'd left me—and he has.

SUSAN: (*Cries out*) No, I won't stay! I'd go mad too if I did.

MRS. M: (*Resigned*) All right, my dear, don't upset yourself. We won't argue. But stay at least until tomorrow. You could never find your way tonight, and besides, if you stay over it will give me a chance to find someone else in town—

SUSAN: I'd rather go now, if you don't mind.

MRS. M: (*Pleading again*) Tomorrow night. Just until then. You may leave after dinner tomorrow. I'll pay you two weeks' wages if you stay until then . . . please . . . you can't refuse me . . .

SUSAN: Well—

MRS. M: Oh, thank you, thank you, dear Susan.

Almost instantly, Susan regrets having agreed to stay. She sleeps badly that night. She is convinced that she hears odd sounds coming from the next room: low chuckles, whispered, voiceless mutterings. But the next day passes uneventfully. When Mrs. Masters returns from the town she tells Susan that a successor has been hired and will arrive the morning after. She spends the late afternoon preparing dinner, informing Susan that she will be free to leave right after it. The old woman takes great pains with the meal, as if preparing a holiday feast. She is an exceedingly gracious hostess all through dinner.

MRS. M: Dear Susan . . . we drink to you . . . my dear, dear Susan . . . to your future . . . to your man . . . (*Laughs*) to your future with your man.

SUSAN: (*Laughs also*) Thank you.

MRS. M: And may you remember this evening all the rest of your days. All the rest—(*Meaningly*)—of your days.

SUSAN: You're very kind.

MRS. M: Not at all, my dear. Let me pour you some more wine. And some for you, John.

SUSAN: Thank you. I'm sorry that I must hurt you by leaving this way. Anything unpleasant I've said I apologize for now. Always, when I think of you, I'll remember this pleasant evening.

MRS. M: (*Colder*) I'm certain of it. And, so that you may remember the better, my dear, let me imprint the occasion still more clearly on your mind. Do you know what it is we celebrate?

SUSAN: (*Puzzled*) I expected it was my leaving.

MRS. M: And so it is. But did it seem likely that you alone would cause so much excitement in my home?

SUSAN: It has been somewhat surprising, I must admit.

MRS. M: No doubt. (*Tensely*) Miss Appleby, this is the third anniversary of the most important event in the history of Masters Hall. We honor you by having you participate.

SUSAN: I'm truly flattered.

MRS. M: I just ask you to listen (*In low, hoarse voice*) Three years ago my son was a genius. Today . . . (*Pause*) he is merely my son. Do you know why? Three years ago the door was slammed on us, locking us apart from the world . . . three years ago tonight. It was slammed by my first companion, a sweet girl like yourself. You see, my son loved her! (*Voice high-pitched, now*) I warned him. I told him. I swore that no woman would put up with his temperament, his moods. He wouldn't listen. He loved her madly. . .(*Laughs hoarsely*) madly. . . the perfect word for it. And for that she slammed the door on him. Slammed it in his face. That very night he lost the power of his mind.

SUSAN: (*Frightened*) I'm sorry. I'm truly sorry. But—

MRS. M: Don't think we've forgotten the occasion, eh, John? (*Grunts of assent*) We've honored it ever since. Two years ago, this evening, on the first anniversary, Sally Thwaite left us. We told her the story . . . she was overwhelmed . . . she couldn't bear to stay. Last year it was another sweet, young companion of mine . . . Katherine . . . Kitty, we called her. She wanted to leave too . . . how could we refuse? And now tonight, Susan Appleby. Tonight you too are leaving us.

SUSAN: (*Fearfully*) Please . . . will you excuse me?

MRS. M: Where are you going, Susan?

SUSAN: To the kitchen . . .

Susan hurries into the kitchen, tries the door. Locked. She believes she is about to be assaulted, murdered, but she cannot know for sure. She thinks of the way the two laugh, especially the old woman fingering her worn, black, ugly shawl. As Susan tries desperately to hit on some plan of escape, Mrs. Masters comes into the kitchen.

MRS. M: Susan, there's one thing more . . . this shawl. So beautiful, so exquisitely wrought; have you noticed it? This shawl belonged to her, that first girl. A gift from my son. (*John appears behind Mrs. Masters*) When she left, it slipped from her shoulders, and I've worn it all the time ever since . . . It's all that remains of that lovely creature. (*Close to Susan*) I should like you to wear it, if only for a moment. (*Grunts of assent from John*) You're so much like her, my dear . . . and the memory of her is John's greatest comfort . . .

SUSAN: (*Screaming*) Don't touch me!

MRS. M: Just around the shoulders? John will like you better that way. He'll give you one little kiss, thinking of *her*. Then he'll play with your hair, as he did with hers. He'll take you upstairs—what's that? Did you hear that? (*Tinkle of front door bell*) Our door! Who would be coming here now? (*Fiercely*) Watch her, John. I'll only be a moment. If she shouts, just choke her . . .

Mrs. Masters, in her shawl, rushes out to the front door, opens it.

MRS. M: Yes. What do you want?

ROB: Pardon me, ma'am. I'm looking for a Miss Susan Appleby.

MRS. M: You won't find her here. I'm sorry.

ROB: Are you certain of that? It seems to me I recognize that shawl. It was worn by the woman Miss Appleby described to me as having hired her.

MRS. M: This isn't the only black shawl in the world, nor am I the only woman who wears one.

ROB: I've been inquiring in town and all the shopkeepers recall you as the woman who *always* does. So I followed you here this morning. Then I returned to town—and now I'm back here again.

MRS. M: Well, isn't that nice! You can turn right around and go back, young man. If you must know, Miss Susan *was* here, but proved so unsatisfactory I sent her packing. You'll probably find her at home right now.

Susan, in the kitchen, has been overhearing all this. Afraid to cry out or move because of John, she starts to whistle, shakily at first, then more clearly, Drink to Me Only with Thine Eyes.

ROB: (*Talking over the whistle*) Well—all right, if she's gone home I'll see her there. Sorry for your trouble (*Leaves*)

John, puzzled by the whistling, has done nothing to stop it. Mrs. Masters slams the front door, runs to the kitchen.

MRS. M: What was that whistling? I thought I told you to be still.

SUSAN: I was nervous. It's a habit of mine.

MRS. M: A bad habit, if you ask me. (*Moves closer*)

SUSAN: Stay away!

MRS. M: Here, now . . . the shawl's around you, see? Draw it tighter, John . . . Tighter!

SUSAN: No! No! (*Tries to scream, but shawl strangles her*)

Suddenly the back door is smashed in.

ROB: You heard her. Arrest her. Watch it—get him, Adams!

MRS. M: Draw, John. Quickly! (*Shot is fired, but by Adams, not John.*) You've killed him. (*Sobbing*) You've killed him . . .

SUSAN: Oh, Rob. You heard me, then?

ROB: Of course . . . You see, this morning I paid a call on our local constabulary and persuaded Adams here to join me.

ADAMS: I was interested, ma'am, because there'd been two disappearances in as many years . . . just about this time . . . and this sounded like a third.

ROB: Darling, I've missed you. I—after her, Adams. Don't let her get out!

They pursue Mrs. Masters, but the old woman escapes the kitchen and locks herself in the parlor. They break down the massive door.

SUSAN: (*Gasps*) Oh, Rob!

ROB: The chandelier . . . Let's cut her down!

ADAMS: Too late. Her neck's gone.

SUSAN: (*Sobs*) Rob . . . Rob . . . she's hanging by the shawl. The old shawl.

NOVELETTE

No possible slip-up; no fuss, no witnesses. You had to hand it to this careful killer

The perfectly

F. HUGH HERBERT

Having completely conquered radio, cinema and stage, the versatile F. Hugh here turns to crime—or rather, returns. For the mystery story is an old love of his, and were his gifts in other directions less demanding, possibly by this time he would have concocted as outstanding a piece in this field as his "Kiss and Tell" was on the stage. It ran on Broadway a mere matter of three years! His most recent play is "The Moon Is Blue," which opened to New York's enthusiastic notices just this past March.

In the warm tale of cold death which you are about to read, Mr. Herbert demonstrates a truly mature pen. The delicate motivation is exceedingly skillful. Each character, even the dead one, lives.

I'VE BEEN QUESTIONED a lot, naturally, but I'm writing this now not under duress. It's simply that I want to put it down on paper. Call it a confession if you want to; a "human document" if you like. It makes no difference, now. Nothing does. Anyway it's the truth, the whole truth. So help me.

Yes—I murdered my wife. Yesterday, Saturday, at about 11:45 A. M. I wasn't crazy then; I don't think I'm crazy now. It just seemed like a good idea at the time. That isn't intended to sound tough or callous or flippant. It's the truth. It's the only explanation I can offer. *It seemed like a hell of a good idea.* Two hours before I killed her I swear I'd never even dreamed of harming her. I had no reason to. I wasn't in love with Connie, I'll admit, and I never had been in love with her, and she knew it, and accepted it, and we always got along fine. We'd been married nearly three years and never once had a fight or even a scene. Matter of fact we managed to have a lot of fun. Certain things she did used to irritate me, but that's only natural in any marriage. I've no doubt lots of things I did irritated her.

I've been wondering, during these past twenty-four hours, whether Con-

calm murder

nie ever thought of killing me. When you've just killed someone you get to wondering about a lot of things. Of course, Connie didn't have to kill me to get rid of me, if she wanted to get rid of me. She could have just kicked me out. I guess that's the difference. I couldn't have kicked her out, at least not on the same terms. . . .

My name is Alan Blake. I'll be twenty-five next October 20th—if I don't go to the gas chamber before then. I married Connie when I was just twenty-two. She said she was thirty-seven at the time, but I think she may have shaded it a couple of years. She'd been married and divorced twice already. It was my first go. I was just out of college.

You see, Connie had a lot of money. I don't know how much, and I never really made any effort to find out, but it was plenty. And Connie was cute. In the right light she could have passed for thirty. She had a good skin, and a cute little figure. She never weighed more than a hundred and five pounds. I always looked older than my age. People knew, of course, that she was older than I, but I don't think they figured it for more than eight or ten years at the most.

Naturally everybody said I married her for her money, and everybody was right. Connie knew it, and I knew it. I'd never had a dime in my life, and I didn't particularly like the idea of working, and then Connie came along, and I guess she fell for me, and it was all very simple. Nobody was kidding anybody. It was a deal, and it suited both of us fine. People gave the marriage six months at best, and said so. Connie didn't give a damn what people said, nor did I. Well, we fooled them about that, anyway. It lasted nearly three years. I don't think Connie ever regretted it. She always seemed perfectly happy. We managed to have a lot of fun.

Connie owned a lot of real estate. We lived in a house she had in Beverly Hills. A small house, but with grounds covering three acres. There's a tennis court, and then, way off beyond the garden, there's a swimming pool and bathhouses surrounded by tall shrubbery. You can't see the pool at all from the house or road. A swell place for sun baths. I like sun bathing better than almost anything else. I guess I was just born lazy.

Yesterday morning I got up about eight. I looked into Connie's room but didn't wake her. I went down to the pool and had a swim, and then I lay around for maybe half an hour and dried off in the sun. Then I walked back to the house in my trunks and asked Vivian to fix me some breakfast and serve it on the patio.

Vivian is Connie's personal maid. We have a couple, too, but yesterday was their day off. Vivian is about twenty-three, I guess, and quite pretty. Most of our so-called "friends" have gone out of their way to tell Connie that she was crazy to hire such a pretty young girl. Meaning with *me* around, of course. Connie always laughed at them. She used to tell me about it. I could see their point, of course. Vivian is really quite cute. But she was crazy about Connie, never more than polite and friendly to me. I never gave the girl a thought, as a woman I mean, and I never stepped out of line for an instant. Nor did she. I just want to make that clear out of fairness to both of us, since Vivian is surely under heavy questioning right now.

I'd finished my ham and eggs, and was reading the paper when Connie finally came down to breakfast on the patio. She was wearing a skimpy, childish, pink playsuit. There was a sort of calculated little-girl quality about it, with a tiny ruffle of lace around the panties and a gingham bow in back. I'd never seen it before, and I didn't like it. That was one of the things about Connie that irritated me. I always wished she wouldn't wear clothes like that. She was tiny, and she had a cute little figure all right, but I always winced when she went cutie-pie in her wardrobe. After all Connie was over forty, and you only had to look at her hands to know it.

Connie took the newspaper away from me and perched herself on my knees. She said: "Hello, darling—sorry I'm late," and then she kissed me on the mouth. I felt uncomfortable. That was another thing about her. There's a time and place for everything. Few people feel amorous at breakfast.

Connie took a napkin, wiped the lipstick from my face, went to her chair and tinkled the little silver bell for Vivian. The girl came in with a small pile of mail. Connie slit the envelopes neatly and deftly with the tip of her forefinger. I sat and watched her hands. They were beautifully groomed, but obviously the hands of a woman past forty. I remember thinking that manicures and cosmetics can't do a thing for a woman's hands. I remember thinking that by contrast with her babyish playsuit, the hands looked even older than they normally did. I remember thinking that I always liked Connie best when we went out at night and she wore gloves.

Connie looked up at me suddenly and, pursing her lips, blew me a kiss. I pretended to catch it somewhere in left field, but again I felt uncomfortable. I wished she wouldn't always try to act cute. I didn't mind so much, funnily enough, when there were others present, because she was small and pretty enough to get away with it. But when we were alone it made me feel uncomfortable. It always seemed so unnecessary.

I guess I must have been frowning because she smiled at me and said: "You look very sleek and gorgeous this morning, Alan—but why so sinister?"

I grinned and told her to cut it out. "Sleek" was one of her favorite adjectives for me, and it always rubbed me the wrong way.

I can remember now, looking back at it, that all these little things were irritating me, making me vaguely uncomfortable, but that was as far as it went at the moment. There had been times, during our marriage, when it had gone a bit further. I'll admit there had been times when I would feel a sudden rush of disgust, almost to the point of hating her. But it had never crystallized into anything. Connie made few enough demands, God knows. And thanks to her I had a home and three servants, a swimming pool, a new Cadillac, a raft of amusing friends. Connie always had a lot of friends. They were nearly all quite wealthy, and much younger than Connie. She liked going around with a young crowd.

Vivian came out onto the patio with the telephone extension and plugged it into the jack. Connie picked up the phone. It was Maureen, a friend of Connie's. Maureen is about twenty, I guess, and pretty. I remember thinking, when I heard Connie speak her name over that phone, that Maureen would look cute in that baby suit of Connie's. She was under contract to some studio for a few months, and they used her all the time for their cheesecake stills.

Connie said that Maureen wanted to come over for a swim and would I like to go and pick her up? Her car was in the shop. I wasn't too keen. I said maybe later I'd think about it. Maureen was around the house quite a lot and I wasn't too keen. Frankly, she bothered me. Too young, too pretty and unscrupulous. And she plays around a lot. At this moment she probably hates my guts. She didn't yesterday. It was one of those things. There was nothing overt, but it was one of those things. A guy can tell. I don't know whether to say that she was on the make for me, or me for her. But it was there. I'm sure Connie had no idea. She was crazy about Maureen, who was always gay and amusing.

Anyway, Connie told her I might pick her up later, and then hung up. Vivian came back onto the patio with Connie's breakfast. She looked pert and pretty in her neat uniform. Connie asked me if we had any dates during the day and when I said no she told Vivian she could have the day off if she wanted to. She was very fond of Vivian.

While they were chatting I got up and stretched myself. The sunlight felt good out there on the patio. I felt good all over. Connie watched me and laughed.

"You do that beautifully," she said. "Doesn't he stretch nicely, Vivian?" I felt like a fool. I think Vivian felt uncomfortable, too. She didn't answer. I could feel my skin prickle with irritation, almost with rage. It was the sort of damn silly remark Connie was always making. She often drew her maid into our conversations, and it always made me feel foolish and uncomfortable. I can't explain why, but it did.

I walked across the patio. The French windows leading to the living room were open. I stepped inside to get a cigarette and then I noticed a large brown stain on the light colored carpet. I came back onto the patio and asked Connie what had happened. She hesitated a moment, and I noticed that she and Vivian exchanged a quick glance.

"A slight domestic accident," Connie said finally. "I spilled a cup of coffee."

I remember thinking that it was nice of Connie to take the rap for her maid, but rather foolish. It was no skin off my nose who spilled the coffee. Vivian wasn't my maid, it wasn't my carpet, and I wasn't paying the bill to have it cleaned.

I'm putting in all this detail for a reason. I'm trying to explain, if only to myself, that I was perfectly rational and calm and logical and normal at that moment. When Connie seemed to be taking the blame for this spilled coffee, I remember thinking that she was always very considerate of people, especially servants. I remember thinking of her with admiration, almost with affection.

I flopped into a chair in the sun and asked Connie whether she had tripped over one of the silly little tables we have in the living room. I was just making conversation. I really didn't give a damn how it had happened. I remember thinking that recently I had always been glad to latch on to any excuse to make casual conversation. Being alone with Connie was making me nervous.

Connie started to answer but before she could get it out Vivian, who was on her way back to the kitchen, turned around suddenly. "Mr. Blake," she said soberly, "Mrs. Blake fainted—that's how come she spilled it. I thought you ought to know about it, Mr. Blake."

She looked at Connie almost apologetically, and then walked off the patio.

Connie was stirring her coffee irritably and I could see she was furious with Vivian.

"Fainted?" I asked. "What does she mean—when did you faint?"

"The girl's a fool," said Connie. "I could wring her neck. I *told* her not to worry you."

I think maybe the whole idea came to me in that moment, but I'm not sure. I asked Connie for details and I remember that I was conscious that my voice sounded quite hoarse and unnatural.

"Oh, Alan," said Connie, "it's so silly. Nothing to worry about, really —I just felt a little dizzy, that's all, and I guess I passed out a few seconds. It's nothing, honestly. The doctor said so."

I asked her when she had spoken to the doctor. I guess the idea must have been forming then already. I remember thinking that Vivian knew about her fainting and I wanted to know for certain whether she'd really checked with the doctor.

Connie said she'd phoned her doctor right away. She said he blamed it on two sets of tennis she had played after a heavy lunch. She said, "Don't look so alarmed, darling—it really doesn't mean anything—it's not the first time I've fainted."

I'm pretty sure the idea was already well under way by then. I remember filing away in my mind the fact that this was not the first time, that this was just one in a series of fainting spells.

I lit another cigarette and I remember that my hands were trembling. I wondered if Connie would notice it. She seemed to and she was concerned about me. She said, "Now Alan, please stop worrying—it was just a little dizzy spell. Ten minutes afterward I felt fine. I went for a swim in the pool."

"You must be crazy," I told her. "If you're given to fainting, for God's sake stay out of the pool."

Connie only smiled at me and told me not to worry.

I got up from my chair in the sun and walked slowly over to the shady side of the patio. By that time the whole idea was working itself out. I could feel my heart pounding against my chest and I remember that I shivered. It was probably ten degrees cooler in the shade but that wasn't why I shivered. I remember thinking that in that instant, moving from sunlight to shadow, I had become a potential murderer. From that moment on I was plotting, planning, building my alibis, considering my defenses, scheming, calculating the risks. From that instant on, in cold blood, on our own patio, I was planning how to murder Connie.

Connie was now dividing her attention between breakfast and the mail. I straddled a chair in the shadow and watched her, fascinated. The sunlight was cruel to her. I could see the tiny lines about her eyes, the myriad tiny little wrinkles that made her silly playsuit so incongruous.

My heart was still pumping noisily but in my mind the plan continued to take shape. The facts and events upon which it was based were fitting neatly into a fascinating pattern.

There was a crazy rhythm to the racing of my heart and I found myself repeating the purpose of my plan to this awful rhythm—*I AM GOING TO MURDER CONNIE—I AM GOING TO MURDER CONNIE—AND I AM GOING TO GET AWAY WITH IT—AWAY WITH IT—AWAY WITH IT.*

I remember distinctly that I pressed my lips together. I was afraid I might be forming the words visibly.

SUDDENLY I became quite calm. My heart ceased pounding. The shocking decision had been made, and now I found I could contemplate my plan and my victim quite dispassionately. I was going to murder Connie but I felt no hatred for her nor, at that moment, even any irritation. I looked at her pretty shoulders and I even felt a sudden rather startling desire for her. . . .

Maybe half an hour later Vivian came out on the patio. She was dressed for the street and asked Connie if she might go now.

From where we live it's quite a a walk to the boulevard. I said I would drive Vivian to the bus. I went to my room and without taking off my swimming trunks I pulled on slacks and a sport shirt.

When I came down Connie was in the hall on her way back to the patio. She asked me again to pick up Maureen and she suggested that maybe I'd like to ask the McAlisters over for a swim. The McAlisters are a young couple whom Connie liked very much. I said sure, it sounded like a good idea.

Then I took the Cadillac and shot Vivian down to the boulevard. There is a bus stop right on the corner but Vivian said she was going somewhere downtown and I said I would drive her part of the way. I had my reasons.

Once we were on Sunset Boulevard heading east I stepped on the gas and pretty soon I was hitting well over seventy. Vivian pointed to the speedometer and warned me that I would probably get a ticket. I smiled. I wanted a ticket.

Pretty soon we heard the familiar wail of a traffic cop's siren and I pulled over to the side of the road. I didn't give the cop any argument. He was a pretty nice guy. I know I was doing over seventy but he put it down on the ticket at fifty. I didn't care. Now I had a beautiful alibi. I told the cop that I was on my way to pick up some friends who were coming up to the house for a swim. We kidded back and forth a minute or so.

I drove Vivian a bit farther. We talked mostly about Connie. I asked her for more details about this fainting spell. She said she'd heard Connie calling the doctor and she kept on telling me not to worry. It was 11:15 by my wrist watch when I dropped Vivian. I turned the car around and drove back to the house. It took me exactly twelve minutes. I remember that it was 11:27 when I pulled the car into the garage.

I found Connie back on the patio still sunning herself. She asked about Maureen and the McAlisters. I told her that I phoned them from a drugstore on the way and that they might be up later in the afternoon.

I said that I was going down to the pool for a swim and Connie jumped up and said she'd come with me. We used to horse around a lot in the pool together and she always enjoyed it. I took off my watch, put it in my pocket, then peeled off slacks and shirt and dived in. Connie went into the bathhouse and changed from her playsuit into a swim suit. It was a bright yellow thing, one of several she kept hanging there.

Connie was a pretty good swimmer. She always used to ask me to stand in the shallow end with my legs apart and then she would dive in and swim under me. Ever since the plan formed in my mind I'd been figuring that she would suggest this now, and she did. I let her swim under my legs maybe three or four times. Each time I moved a little nearer to the edge. I had to have something against which to brace myself.

I think it was the fourth time when I put the plan into execution. As she was swimming under water between my legs I put my foot on the back of her neck and held her under water against the tile bottom of the pool. I had figured it well—by shifting only slightly I was able to put both feet across her neck and shoulders, and I could bear down firmly, getting leverage from the rail around the pool. Really nothing to it. I remember thinking it was too simple. I felt no emotion at all, no guilt, no horror, no excitement, no remorse. I was doing a job I'd planned, and doing it efficiently.

Her arms were spread-eagled on the bottom of the pool and I was able to exert enough pressure to prevent her from reaching her arms up. She couldn't move. She was pinned down there, firmly. Her face was pressed against the bottom of the pool and the only sound you could hear was the bubbles coming up. For a few moments her legs were thrashing around but pretty soon they became lifeless. Maybe she fainted again. I don't know. I hope so. I remember hoping that she wasn't suffering. I knew she must be, but I hoped she wasn't. She looked very tiny in her yellow swimming suit.

The bubbles kept rising for a long time. It may have been five minutes. I don't know. I remember thinking that I'd have to be very careful not to apply too much pressure. I didn't want any bruises or marks on her. Connie always bruised easily. She had a lovely skin.

Finally, maybe a minute after the last bubble came up, I took one foot off her neck and then the other. I wasn't sure what was going to happen. I didn't know if the body would stay under water or float to the top. I was perfectly calm. I climbed out of the pool. She looked like a small yellow flower lying there under the water. I waited to see what would happen. Nothing happened. Her body remained lying on the bottom of the pool, absolutely motionless.

I picked up slacks, shirt, shoes and socks and went into the bathhouse. I was perfectly calm. I took a shower and dressed.

When I came out Connie's body still hugged the bottom of the pool. I looked at my wrist watch. It was exactly 11:45. I took out my wallet and looked at the ticket the speed cop had given me. He had written down the time, 11:05. Not a perfect alibi, of course. But plausible.

We live on a winding street where there are few houses, and these set well back. I had noticed very carefully, riding back, that no pedestrians had seen me return. I got into the Cadillac again and drove away. There was no traffic and I'm sure that not a soul saw me. I knew I was safe. I tore down the boulevard and turned west. During the actual killing I'd been perfectly calm. Now, when I thought I'd gotten away with it, I was beginning to get the shakes. Driving out towards the ocean along Sunset, I needed a drink in the worst way but was afraid to stop anywhere. I didn't want any bartender to remember afterwards that I had come in for a brandy. I didn't want to take any chances.

I drove as quickly as I thought safe and I forced myself to calm down. Pretty soon I was okay again.

I remember quite distinctly figuring up just how I stood at that moment. It looked solid. Not only Vivian but the doctor knew that Connie was subject to these fainting spells. When they found her body in the pool they'd naturally assume she had passed out again and had drowned. The servants were all out and there wasn't anyone else even within shouting distance.

I remember figuring that in all these cases they nearly always suspect the husband but that didn't worry me. I had an alibi—from the police department itself. I was ten miles away from our home, still heading away from home, only forty minutes before she was drowned. Both the speed cop and Vivian knew from me that I was on my way to round up Maureen and the McAlisters. If necessary they'd testify to this effect.

I wasn't worried either that the police or the D. A.'s office could dig up any motive. Everyone knew that Connie and I got along fine. Vivian would testify that I really was very much concerned when she mentioned about the fainting. The McAlisters live in Westwood. I planned to stop by their house first and then pick up Maureen later, but this wasn't necessary. I found Maureen with them. She had phoned and told them her car was on the blink and Bert McAlister had picked her up. I told them all that Connie was waiting up at the house, and would they like to come up for a swim? The McAlisters don't have a pool and they were all for it. I stayed there for maybe ten minutes and had a drink.

We left in the two cars. Maureen said she had nothing to do all day and figured she might stay and have dinner with us. The McAlisters had a date later on. Maureen got into my car and the McAlisters followed us.

Maureen asked me how Connie felt and I said fine. Maureen said, "The reason I ask is because I called her the other day and she told me that she just had passed out or something."

I told Maureen it was nothing, or at least that Connie had said it was nothing. I was very casual about it. I was glad she had mentioned it, though. It strengthened my case. Now Maureen, and possibly others, knew about Connie's fainting spells.

I steered my car into the garage, next to Connie's Lincoln convertible. The McAlisters parked in front of the house. We went in through a side door that leads directly onto the patio.

They came onto the patio behind me and when they saw that Connie wasn't there Doris McAlister looked up at the window of Connie's bedroom and yelled, "Hey, Connie, come on down; we're here."

Bert said he'd welcome a drink and Maureen, who likes her liquor, said she'd take one also. I told them that I'd have to be bartender since the help were all out, and I went into the kitchen.

When I came back with the drinks Doris was just coming out through the French windows from the living room. She said, "Connie isn't in the house. I just went up to her room."

Bert, who was lying on a chaise-longue smoking a cigarette, suggested that maybe Connie had gone out somewhere.

Maureen said, "Not unless someone picked her up. I saw her car in the garage."

It was Maureen who suggested that maybe Connie had gone down to the pool. Somehow I had figured all along that she would think of that—I don't know why.

Bert grinned and said, "Maybe she's swimming in the nude—let's go and surprise her." They knew that we went into the pool without swimming suits. It was that secluded.

We sat around for a few minutes and finished our drinks. It was all very casual and leisurely. Nobody was at all concerned about Connie's absence.

I was busy figuring out the next step. I pretended to be busy over the tray of drinks but I was figuring everything very carefully. I decided to let the others go ahead and find her body first. I was going to bring up in the rear carrying a big tray of drinks and when I heard the first cry I would drop the tray with a loud crash. I'd figured out even details like that.

While I was still stalling over the tray Maureen nudged me and pointed. She said, "Look, Alan—there's a rainbow from the spray."

I can't think how I had failed to notice it before. The sprinklers were on now. *But they had not been on when I'd left!* Or so it seemed to me. I was positive that the sprinklers had not been on; and yet, could I be absolutely sure? I tried desperately to recall every move I had made after climbing out of the pool. Every detail was vivid in my mind, but I couldn't remember the sprinklers.

My heart began pounding my ribs again. I wondered if the gardener could possibly have been there. I knew he never came on Saturdays. I couldn't figure it out. I think I must have hypnotized myself into believing that I myself must have turned them on before I'd left. I stopped being panicky. I was calm again. I looked at the rainbow in the spray, and I remember thinking it was pretty.

Finally Maureen said, "It's so damn hot up here—let's go down to the pool."

She led the way. The McAlisters followed. I said, "Go on ahead—I'll have to get this tray ready."

I remember distinctly that my voice sounded perfectly calm and normal.

I let them get well ahead of me and then followed, keeping my eyes on the tray.

I was holding my breath waiting for the first horrified shriek. I heard Doris say cheerfully, "You know, this is the nicest pool in Beverly Hills."

I stood there shaking, and the glasses on the tray danced insanely. I figured that maybe they hadn't looked into the pool, but that didn't seem reasonable because it's not a big pool anyway and the water is always as clear as crystal.

I heard the noisy creaking of the glider as someone sat down on it. I couldn't stand it any longer. My knees were like water but I somehow managed to walk up to the others.

Maureen was swinging gently in the glider. Bert and Doris were sitting on chairs by the edge of the pool. There was no sign of Connie's body. The sun was beating down and there wasn't even a wet mark around the edge of the pool. It had disappeared.

I set the heavy tray down on the table and I stared at the pool. I had never been so frightened or horrified in my life.

MAUREEN and the others after a moment or two went into the bathhouses to change. For what seemed like hours, but probably was only a minute or two, I couldn't think of anything. I just stared at the pool—stared at the spot where I had drowned Connie. I was in a sweat and I shook all over.

Then suddenly I linked it up. The sprinklers! Pancho *must* have come after I'd gone. He comes twice a week and he had been there the day before. I had taken that fact into consideration. He wasn't due for another three days and yet I realized that for some technical gardening reason he must have come to turn on the sprinklers and found her body in the pool. I cursed Pancho's eternal soul.

I became very calm again. This hadn't really killed my plan. I would merely have to change it a bit. I remember saying this to myself: *You know nothing about it—you don't know anything. You left her on the patio, that's all you know—You've no idea that she's dead—You've no idea how she met her death—you know nothing.*

Doris, Bert and Maureen came out of the bathhouses in a bunch and dived into the pool together. They splashed around and laughed. I sat down on a chair near the table. Maureen swam over to me. She said, "Come on, slowpoke, get into your trunks."

My voice sounded normal. I said I didn't think I'd swim. Maureen said, "Oh, come on. I'll kiss you under water like they do in those swim suit advertisements."

I couldn't bear the thought of getting into the pool. I said I'd fix drinks for them and go in later.

Doris said, "What's the matter—don't you feel well?"

Bert told Maureen that he'd like to try that kissing under water and they went at it. Bubbles came up. I felt sick. I remember thinking that bubbles from kissing shouldn't look like bubbles from dying.

Doris suggested that I might phone a few people to try to locate Connie. She was convinced that somebody had come by and picked her up in their car.

We have a telephone extension down at the bathhouse. I called up a few of our friends and asked if they had seen Connie by any chance. When the others happened to be near they listened to the conversation and once or twice someone took the phone out of my hand and talked to these friends. It was all very casual. Nobody was concerned. They all figured that Connie would blow in any minute.

The McAlisters stayed well over an hour. They had a few more drinks, then told me to say hello to Connie for them and went to keep their date.

I walked back to the house to see them into their car and Maureen in her wet suit tagged along. She said she was going into the pool again. I didn't want her to stay but there was nothing I could do about it.

After they had gone Maureen and I remained on the patio. I looked at my watch. It was a few minutes before three. I knew that it couldn't be very long before the phone or doorbell would ring and I would have to answer a lot of questions. I was still quite calm. I figured I could still get away with it if I just remembered that I knew absolutely nothing about anything. I was quite ready for almost every question.

I sat in a comfortable chair and Maureen stretched herself out on the hot tiles at my feet and sunned herself. Once she raised her head lazily, pursed up her lips and blew me a kiss. It was exactly what Connie had done a few hours earlier. I lit a cigarette and told Maureen to cut it out. She looked rather startled.

While I was in the kitchen getting some White Rock I heard a car pull up and a moment later the front doorbell rang. I knew instinctively that this was it. I finished fixing a highball for myself and I went to the front door holding the glass in one hand. I had myself under good control. My hand wasn't shaking in the least. I remember looking at my hand, and feeling very pleased that it was so steady.

A DAPPER little man with a neat brown mustache was standing on the threshold. He wore a light Palm Beach suit and a Panama hat. He didn't look like a cop but I knew that he must be. He said, "Are you Alan Blake?" and he started groping in his hip pocket for a wallet. I said, "Yes, I'm Blake." I let him stand on the threshold. I didn't ask him in. I pretended I had no idea who he was or what he might want. I was going to let him carry the ball. I was polite but rather cool. I think I put on a pretty good act.

He showed me a badge and said, "I'm Mowbray of the Homicide Squad." I still stood at the door, holding my drink, and I made no move to invite him in. I said, "Yes?" and I remember thinking that I got just the right inflection of puzzled surprise into the query.

Mowbray has large, brown, friendly and even kindly eyes. He never took them off me for an instant. I looked at him quite steadily. He has a pleasant voice too. Low-pitched, and well educated. I don't remember his exact words but finally he said something to the effect that he had bad news for me and that it was about my wife, and might he come in.

I yelped, "My wife—what do you mean—what happened?" and led him into the living room. In a friendly way he suggested that maybe I had better sit down. I sat on the piano bench.

Mowbray circled the living room once, slowly. I think he noticed everything. He looked down at the stain where Connie had dropped the coffee and then he looked out on the patio and saw Maureen there. He closed the French windows. Then he walked over to the piano and from the breast pocket of his coat took a small notebook. A frayed old notebook, held together by red rubber bands. There was a stub of pencil stuck under the bands. He looked at me steadily and, it seemed to me, rather sympathetically. Finally I said, "What *about* my wife; what happened? I came back about an hour-and-a-half ago and she'd gone out—what happened?"

He said, very quietly, "Mr. Blake, your wife is dead. We have her down at the morgue."

While I was fixing the drink for myself in the kitchen just before Mowbray came I had already anticipated this moment. I did now just what I planned to do. I jumped up and stared at him in horror. I yelled, "Dead! My God, what do you mean—what happened?"

I must have yelled pretty loud. Maureen opened the French windows, pushed into the room. She said, "Alan, what's wrong?"

I remember wishing to heaven that she hadn't come up to the house in the first place. She'd been lying out in the patio sunning herself, and she'd lowered the straps of her swimming suit off her shoulders, and now when she barged in she hadn't bothered to raise them. I remember thinking that she looked too damn pretty. I remember thinking that she looked like a good motive for a murder. I remember wondering whether I had really murdered Connie so that I could have Maureen. I said, "This man is from the Homicide Bureau. It's about Connie. Something's happened. She's dead."

Maureen sat down slowly on the arm of a chair. She started to cry. She said, "Oh, no—no!" She looked at me. Her eyes were full of terror. Maybe she guessed what had happened. I don't know.

I told Mowbray who Maureen was and he asked me quietly to take her out of the room. I did what he told me.

As soon as I came back he started asking me questions. He said they were just routine questions always asked in these cases and his manner was still friendly and sympathetic.

I don't think I was really nervous. I kept on repeating to myself: *"You know nothing . . . you're innocent . . . you know absolutely nothing."*

I kept on saying, "My God—what happened? How did it happen?" but Mowbray always managed to avoid a direct answer. I didn't know whether to ask him specifically how Connie had died or to wait until he told me. I wondered what an innocent man would have done, but I couldn't be sure. I was getting jumpy and confused.

Finally Mowbray opened the notebook and started asking real questions. He asked me when was the last time I saw Connie alive. I had the answer to that all pat. I told him that I drove the maid into Hollywood and that it must have been about ten minutes of eleven when I left. He wrote that down and he asked me if I could be sure of the time.

I said, "Yes, I can, more or less. It so happens I got a ticket for speeding about fifteen minutes later."

I pulled out my wallet and showed him the ticket. I said, "You'll see that the time is written on there and also where I was when the cop had me pull over."

He studied the ticket carefully and made notes. I wanted to bite out my tongue. I realized immediately that I had been much too eager and glib about offering this alibi. From then on I answered his questions far more carefully. I was purposely vague. I figured that an innocent man would be terribly confused.

Mowbray quietly asked where I had gone after getting the ticket. I told him that I dropped Vivian somewhere in Hollywood. I said I couldn't remember exactly what corner but that Vivian might. I explained that Connie had given her the day off and that she wouldn't be back until late that night.

Mowbray said, "And where did you go after that, Mr. Blake?"

I told him that my wife had wanted me to pick up some friends to come and swim. I told him I couldn't remember exactly what time it was when I got to the McAlisters. I explained that they had left just a little while ago and that Maureen had decided to stick around and wait for Connie. I gave him the names of some of the people I called when I was pretending to check on where Connie might be. He asked for the telephone numbers and I gave him one or two. I said I couldn't remember the others. I said I was too upset.

He wrote it all down in his little book.

I guess I must have been staring at the coffee stain because I remember he asked me about that. I told him Connie had spilled a cup of coffee a few days ago. I didn't know whether to say anything about her fainting. I decided not to. If it came up later I could tell all about it. I could say that I was too upset to remember at the time.

Mowbray said, "Mr. Blake, when you left this morning at ten minutes of eleven, where was your wife?" I told him she said she was going back to the patio to finish breakfast. He asked if I could remember what she was wearing. I described Connie's pink playsuit. I told him I remembered it so vividly because it had irritated me. He wrote it down.

He kept on asking questions. I didn't like the sound of it. He wanted to know did we get along all right, had we had a fight recently; things like that. He was no longer quite as friendly and compassionate as he had been. I was beginning to get rattled. Suddenly I couldn't take it any more.

I said, "Look, what are you driving at? Why are you asking me all these questions?"

He flipped over a new page in his notebook and sucked his stub of pencil. He said, "Just routine, Mr. Blake. I realize they must be harrowing." He was quite apologetic.

He asked me Connie's age. I told him I thought she was forty, but I couldn't be quite sure; I'd never seen her birth certificate. He asked my age and when I told him he raised his eyebrows and said, "That's very interesting."

And immediately he started asking questions about Maureen; how old was she; did she come to the house often; where did she live, and so on. He asked was she my friend or Connie's? How long had we known her? I can't remember all the questions. He had already asked me what time it was when I got back to the house with the McAlisters and Maureen. Now he suddenly said, "Between the time you left the house this morning and *that* time, Mr. Blake, did you by any chance come back to the house for any reason?"

I was prepared for that one. I said, "No, of course not."

"You were pretty slow getting to your friends and bringing them back here."

I explained that, having just caught one ticket for speeding, I'd wanted to avoid getting another. He made a note of it all. I remember distinctly that from this point on I was getting more and more rattled. I was annoyed with myself because I hadn't stopped in somewhere on the way to the beach for a cup of coffee or even a drink. It would have been a good alibi. I could sense that Mowbray rather doubted my story. Over and over he asked me to repeat what time I left the house.

Finally I yelled at him, "Look—for God's sake—instead of rehashing all this stuff why won't you tell me what happened! How did she die? You haven't even told me *that* yet!"

He said, "Of course, Mr. Blake. I'm sorry. Death was by drowning. Mrs. Blake's body was found in the swimming pool by your gardener. He notified the police. We're holding him for further questioning."

My heart pounded in my ears and in my throat. At last it was out in the open. I didn't have to pretend not to know. I said, "My God—it's impossible. She was a good swimmer."

He made a note of that. He asked if she were a good diver. I said she was pretty good.

He started asking me questions about Pancho, the gardener. He wanted to know how long Pancho had worked for us, whether we considered him trustworthy, stuff like that. I got the definite idea he thought Pancho might have had something to do with it. I asked what time Pancho had found Connie in the pool. Mowbray looked in his notebook and told me they weren't sure. He said: "The man has no watch and says he didn't know the exact time."

My heart was still pounding. I figured the cops suspected something wasn't quite kosher and might try to hang it on Pancho. I told Mowbray that I was surprised to hear Pancho had been at the house. I explained that he'd been here yesterday and wasn't due to come again until Monday. I felt like a heel, but hell, it was Pancho or me. Mowbray wrote it all down. He seemed to be eating it up.

I felt it reasonably safe now to ask for more details. Mowbray was quite willing to give them. He moistened his thumb and flipped back a number of pages in his notebook. In a dull, droning voice he read a rambling statement that Pancho had made. He told me they had questioned the man pretty thoroughly. He said Pancho had told them he was once in jail. I never knew that. I doubt if Connie knew it. I remember him reading this: "Question: Have you ever heard Mr. and Mrs. Blake quarreling? Answer: Sure—they fight once in a while. Nothing bad." I was furious. I told Mowbray it was a damned lie, which it was. We had never quarreled, not once.

Here Mowbray interrupted suddenly to ask me if we'd ever had any trouble with Pancho. I remembered that Connie had bawled him out once about some camellia bushes that died. It made Pancho sore and he hadn't come back to work for a week. I told Mowbray about it. He wrote it down. He asked me if Pancho had ever tried to get fresh with Connie or with Vivian. I didn't answer immediately. Then I said that I'd never actually noticed anything specific. Mowbray asked me what I meant by that. I said I didn't like the way Pancho used to look at Connie sometimes. I said it might have been my imagination. I'd never spoken about it.

Mowbray went back to his book and started reading from Pancho's questioning. I was feeling better all the time. I was still elated by the knowledge that Pancho had been in jail, and that the cops knew about it. It seemed like a break for me.

I remember Mowbray reading this: "Question: When you saw the body of Mrs. Blake in the pool what did you do? Answer: I pulled her out. She was in the shallow end. Question: Then what did you do? Answer: I put a big towel over her. She had nothing on."

I said, "He's a liar. She had on a yellow suit." Then I bit my tongue so hard that I've been tasting blood ever since. I stared at Mowbray, who glanced up from his notebook and looked at me for a long time. Very quietly he said, "You interrupted me, Mr. Blake." He turned back to his notebook and went on reading. He read, "Question: You mean that she was naked? Answer: No, I didn't mean that. She had on a little yellow swimming suit which was practically nothing."

Mowbray closed his notebook and snapped the rubber bands around it. He said, very quietly, "Mr. Blake, you told us a couple of times that when you last saw your wife she was wearing a pink playsuit. How did you know she died in a yellow suit?"

That was a question I couldn't answer. I couldn't think. I heard nothing but the pounding of my heart. I remember feeling horribly embarrassed. Fear came later, and horror and remorse. Right then all I could feel was a sickening sense of shame at my stupidity for jumping the gun.

Now he had asked the jackpot question and I had no answer prepared for *that*. I couldn't speak. I could only taste the blood in my mouth.

a horseman in the sky

He glimpsed a strange enemy in his rifle sight. Should he squeeze the trigger?

AMBROSE BIERCE

Of all the breeders of suspense, war is probably the most prolific. Yet compelling war stories are scarce in the short literature of our day. Ambrose Bierce, of course, knew no master at telling war's tense, bitter tale; were he writing today no doubt our public prints would be the richer for such content. There's some hope, too, that he may resume. Although he disappeared mysteriously in 1914, periodic rumors hold him still alive in South America. This would make him, at the moment, approximately 109 years old.

ONE SUNNY afternoon in Autumn of 1861 a soldier lay in a laurel clump by the side of a road in western Virginia. He lay at full length upon his stomach, feet resting on the toes, head on his left forearm. His extended right hand loosely grasped his rifle. But for the somewhat methodical disposition of his limbs and a slight rhythmic movement of the cartridge-box at the back of his belt he might have been thought dead. He was asleep at his post of duty. If detected he would be dead enough shortly afterward, death being the just and legal penalty for his crime.

The clump of laurel in which the criminal lay was in the angle of a road which after climbing from the south to that point turned sharply to the west, running along a summit for perhaps one hundred yards. There it turned southward again and went zigzagging downward through the forest. A great rock capped the high cliff; a stone dropped from its outer edge would have fallen sheer downward one thousand feet to the tops of the pines. The angle where the soldier lay was on another spur of the same cliff. Had he been awake he would have commanded a view not only of the short arm of the road and the jutting rock, but of the entire profile of the cliff below it. It might well have made him giddy to look.

The country was wooded everywhere except at the bottom of the valley to the northward, where there was a small natural meadow, through which flowed a stream scarcely visible from the valley's rim. This open ground looked hardly larger than an ordinary dooryard, but was really several acres in extent. Its green was more vivid than that of the inclosing forest. Away beyond it rose a line of giant cliffs similar to those through which the road had somehow made its climb to the summit.

No country is so wild and difficult but men will make it a theatre of war; concealed in the forest at the bottom of that military rat-trap, in which half a hundred men in possession of the exits might have starved an army to submission, lay five regiments of Federal infantry. They had marched all the previous day and night and were resting. At nightfall they would take to the road again, climb to the place where their unfaithful sentinel now slept, and descending the other slope of the ridge fall upon a camp of the enemy at about midnight. Their hope was to surprise it, for the road led to the rear of it. In case of failure, their position would be perilous in the extreme; and fail they surely would should accident or vigilance apprise the enemy of the movement.

The sleeping sentinel in the clump of laurel was a young Virginian named Carter Druse. He was the only child of wealthy parents, and had known such ease and cultivation and high living as wealth and taste were able to command in the mountain country of western Virginia. His home was but a few miles from where he now lay. One morning he had risen from the breakfast table and said, quietly but gravely: "Father, a Union regiment has arrived at Grafton. I am going to join it."

The father lifted his leonine head, looked at the son a moment in silence, and replied: "Well, go, sir, and whatever may occur do what you conceive to be your duty. Virginia, to which you are a traitor, must go on without you. Should we both live to the end of the war, we will speak further of the matter. Your mother, as the physician has informed you, is in a most critical condition; at the best she cannot be with us longer than a few weeks, but that time is precious. Best not to disturb her."

So Carter Druse, bowing reverently to his father, who returned the salute with a stately courtesy that masked a breaking heart, left the home of his childhood to go soldiering. By conscience and courage, he soon commended himself to his fellows and it was to these qualities and to some knowledge of the country that he owed his selection for his present perilous duty at the extreme outpost. Nevertheless, fatigue had been stronger than resolution and he had fallen asleep. What good or bad angel came in a dream to rouse him from his state of crime, who shall say? Without a movement, without a sound, in the profound silence and the languor of the late afternoon, some invisible messenger of fate whispered the mysterious awakening word. He quietly raised his forehead and looked between the masking stems of the laurel.

His first feeling was of keen artistic delight. On a colossal pedestal, the cliff—motionless at the extreme edge of the capping rock and sharply outlined against the sky—was an equestrian statue of impressive dignity. The figure of a man sat the figure of the horse, straight and soldierly, but with the repose of a Grecian god carved in the marble which limits the suggestion of activity. The gray costume harmonized with its aerial background; the metal of accoutrement and caparison was softened and subdued by the shadow across the pommel of the saddle. In silhouette against the sky the profile of the horse was cut with the sharpness of a cameo; it looked across the heights of air to the confronting cliffs beyond. The face of the rider, turned slightly away, showed only an outline of temple and beard; he was looking downward to the bottom of the valley. Magnified by its lift against the sky and by the soldier's testifying sense of the formidableness of a near enemy, the group appeared of heroic, almost colossal, size.

For an instant Druse had a strange, half-defined feeling that he had slept to the end of the war and was looking upon a noble work of art reared upon that eminence to commemorate the deeds of an heroic past of which he had been an inglorious part. The feeling was dispelled by a slight movement of the group; the horse, without moving its feet, had drawn its body slightly backward from the verge; the man remained immobile as before. Broad awake and keenly alive to the significance of the situation, Druse now brought the butt of his rifle against his cheek by cautiously pushing the barrel forward through the bushes, cocked the piece, and glancing through the sights covered a vital spot of the horseman's breast. A touch upon the trigger and all would have been well with Carter Druse. At that instant the horseman turned his head and looked in the direction of his concealed foeman—seemed to look into his very face, into his eyes, into his brave, compassionate heart.

Is it then so terrible to kill an enemy in war—an enemy who has surprised a secret vital to the safety of one's self and comrades—an enemy more formidable for his knowledge than all his army for its numbers? Carter Druse grew pale; he shook in every limb, turned faint. His hand fell away from his weapon. This hardy soldier was near swooning from intensity of emotion.

But not for long; in another moment his face was raised from earth, his hands resumed their places on the rifle; his forefinger sought the trigger; mind, heart, and eyes were clear, conscience and reason sound. He could not hope to capture that enemy; to alarm him would but send him dashing to his camp with his fatal news. The duty of the soldier was plain: the man must be shot dead from ambush—without warning, without a moment's spiritual preparation, with never so much as an unspoken prayer, he must be sent to his account. But no—there is a hope; he may have discovered nothing—perhaps he is but admiring the sublimity of the landscape. If permitted, he may turn and ride carelessly away in the direction whence he came. Surely it will be possible to judge at the instant of his withdrawing whether he knows. It may well be that his fixity of attention—Druse turned his head and looked through the deeps of air downward, as from the surface to the bottom of a translucent sea. He saw creeping across the green meadow a sinuous line of figures of men and horses—some foolish commander was permitting the soldiers of his escort to water their beasts in the open, in plain view from a dozen summits!

Druse withdrew his eyes from the valley and fixed them again upon the group of man and horse in the sky, and again it was through the sights of his rifle. But this time his aim was at the horse. In his memory, as if they were a divine mandate, rang the words of his father at their parting: "Whatever may occur, do what you conceive to be your duty." He was calm now. His teeth were firmly but not rigidly closed; his nerves were as tranquil as a sleeping babe's—not a tremor affected any muscle of his body; his breathing, until suspended in the act of taking aim, was regular and slow. Duty had conquered; the spirit had said to the body: "Peace, be still." He fired.

An officer of the Federal force, who in a spirit of adventure or in quest of knowledge had left the hidden *bivouac* in the valley, and with aimless feet had made his way to the lower edge of a small open space near the foot of the cliff, was considering what he had to gain by pushing his exploration further. At a distance of a quarter-mile before him, but apparently at a stone's throw, rose from its fringe of pines the gigantic face of rock, towering to so great a height above him that it made him giddy to look up to where its edge cut a sharp, rugged line against the sky. It presented a clean, vertical profile against a background of blue sky to a point half the way down, and of distant hills, hardly less blue, thence to the tops of the trees at its base. Lifting his eyes to the dizzy altitude of its summit the officer saw an astonishing sight—a man on horseback riding down into the valley through the air!

Straight upright sat the rider, in military fashion, with a firm seat in the saddle, a strong clutch upon the rein to hold his charger from too impetuous a plunge. From his bare head his long hair streamed upward, waving like a plume. His hands were concealed in the cloud of the horse's lifted mane. The animal's body was as level as if every hoof-stroke encountered the resistant earth. Its motions were those of a wild gallop, but even as the officer looked they ceased, with all the legs thrown sharply forward as in the act of alighting from a leap.

But this was a flight!

Filled with amazement and terror by this apparition of a horseman in the sky—half believing himself the chosen scribe of some new Apocalypse—the officer was overcome by the intensity of his emotions; his legs failed him and he fell. Almost at the same instant he heard a crashing sound in the trees—a sound that died without an echo—and all was still.

The officer rose to his feet, trembling. Pulling himself together he ran obliquely away from the cliff to a point distant from its foot; thereabout he expected to find his man; and thereabout he naturally failed. In the fleeting instant of his vision his imagination had been so wrought upon by the apparent grace and ease and intention of the marvelous performance that it did not occur to him that the line of march of aerial cavalry is directly downward, and that he could find the objects of his search at the very foot of the cliff. A half-hour later he returned to camp.

This officer was a wise man; he knew better than to tell an incredible truth. He said nothing of what he had seen. But when the commander asked him if in his scout he had learned anything of advantage to the expedition he answered:

"Yes, sir; there is no road leading down into this valley from the south."

The commander, knowing better, smiled.

After firing his shot, Private Carter Druse reloaded his rifle and resumed his watch. Ten minutes had hardly passed when a Federal sergeant crept cautiously to him on hands and knees. Druse neither turned his head nor looked at him, but lay without motion or sign of recognition.

"Did you fire?" the sergeant whispered.

"Yes."

"At what?"

"A horse. It was standing on yonder rock—pretty far out. You see it is no longer there. It went over the cliff."

The man's face was white, but he showed no other sign of emotion. Having answered, he turned away his eyes and said no more. The sergeant did not understand.

"See here, Druse," he said, after a moment's silence, "it's no use making a mystery. I order you to report. Was there anybody on the horse?"

"Yes."

"Well?"

"My father."

The sergeant rose to his feet and walked away. "Good God!" he said.

FOR HIGH-TENSION READING

. . . that will keep you on the edge of your seat!

Outstanding fiction by the leading practitioners of the art of curdling your blood, curling your hair and chilling your spine.

Five kinds of thrilling stories

SCIENCE-FICTION • MYSTERY • FANTASY • CRIME • ADVENTURE

all combined in one tension-packed magazine.

BARGAIN SUBSCRIPTION OFFER

Subscribe now to SUSPENSE Magazine to assure you of prompt delivery of this five-variety chiller-diller story teller. It's yours at the bargain rate of $1.00 for four issues (regular newsstand price would be $1.40—you save 40c). Just fill in the coupon, pin a dollar, check or money-order to it, and you are in for hours of adventurous reading.

• •

SUSPENSE MAGAZINE Subscription Dep't. E2
420 Lexington Avenue,
New York 17, N. Y.

Here's my dollar for the bargain offer of 4 issues of SUSPENSE Magazine. Start my subscription with the Winter number.

Name____

Address____

City____________________ Zone_____ State________________

The Fiction House Press Replica Line is available at www.FictionHousePress.com

—Continued from back cover

www.ingramcontent.com/pod-product-compliance
Lightning Source LLC
LaVergne TN
LVHW091005080826
845145LV00003B/1131